The Firsts in Life

Aaron Abilene

Published by Syphon Creative, 2024.

THE FIRSTS IN LIFE

First edition. November 6, 2024.

Copyright © 2024 Aaron Abilene.

ISBN: 979-8223216681

Written by Aaron Abilene.

Also by Aaron Abilene

Afterlife in Love

Island
Paradise Island
The Lost Island
The Lost Island 2
The Island 2

Pandemic
Pandemic

Prototype
The Compound

Slacker
Slacker 2
Slacker: Dead Man Walkin'

Texas
A Vampire in Texas

Thomas
Quarantine

Contagion
Eradication
Isolation

Zombie Bride
Zombie Bride
Zombie Bride 2
Zombie Bride 3

Standalone
The Victims of Pinocchio
A Christmas Nightmare
Pain
Fat Jesus
A Zombie's Revenge
505
The Headhunter
Crash
Tranq
The Island
Dog
The Quiet Man
Joe Superhero
Feral
Good Guys
Devil Child of Texas
Romeo and Juliet and Zombies
The Gamer
Becoming Alpha
Dead West

Small Town Blues
The Gift of Death
Killer Claus
Home Sweet Home
Alligator Allan
10 Days
Army of The Dumbest Dead
Kid
The Cult of Stupid
9 Time Felon
Slater
Me Again
Maurice and Me
Sparkles The Vampire Clown
She's Psycho
Vicious Cycle
Romeo and Juliet: True Love Conquers All
Random Acts of Stupidity
The Abducted
Graham Hiney
The Firsts in Life

The Firsts in Life

Written by Aaron Abilene

Charlie prays.

Charlie on his knees beside his bed "Dear god , I'm Charlie, it's okay if you forgot about me, I know everyone else did."

Cont.

Charlie: "God, I just wanted to ask you for a favor."

Cont.

Charlie: "I want you to show me that you are real."

Cont.

Charlie: "I want you to show me what my purpose is in this life, I am depressed and I don't know where else to turn."

Charlie felt tears streaming down his face as he waited for an answer. He wasn't sure if he actually believed in God, but with everything that had been happening lately, he figured it couldn't hurt to try. As he knelt there in silence, he suddenly felt a gust of wind blow through the room and the hairs on the back of his neck stood up.

Thinking it was just a draft, Charlie opened his eyes, only to see a figure standing at the end of his bed. It was tall and imposing, with features that Charlie couldn't quite make out. Slowly, it began to walk towards him, and as it drew closer, Charlie could see that it was wearing a long black cloak that seemed to billow out behind it like wings.

"Who are you?" Charlie whispered, feeling a lump rise in his throat.

"I am the guardian of purpose," the figure replied in a deep voice that echoed throughout the room. "I have come to show you your true path."

Charlie watched as the figure extended its bony hand towards him. Hesitantly, he took it, feeling a jolt of energy course through his body as soon as their skin touched.

"You are meant to do great things," the guardian said. "But you must first overcome your own doubts and fears."

With that, the figure vanished into thin air, leaving behind a sense of clarity and determination in Charlie's mind. For the first time in months, he felt hope for his future.

As Charlie finished his prayer, he sat back on his heels and looked up at the ceiling, waiting for a sign, a glimmer of hope. But nothing came. The room remained silent and still. He sighed and brushed away a tear that had escaped his eye.

Suddenly, a faint whisper echoed through the room. Charlie's heart raced as he strained to listen. Again, the whisper came, a little louder this time.

"Charlie," it said.

Charlie's eyes widened in shock as he realized the voice was coming from within him. It was his own voice, but it sounded different, as if someone else was speaking through him.

"You are not forgotten," the voice continued. "You are loved, and your life has purpose."

Charlie's mind raced with questions, but before he could ask anything, the voice spoke again.

"Your purpose is to bring love and light into the world. You have a gift for writing that can touch people's hearts and inspire them to greatness."

As the voice trailed off, Charlie felt a warmth inside him that he had never known before. He wiped away another tear with newfound hope.

"Thank you," Charlie whispered to himself, knowing that he was not alone in this world after all.

As Charlie finished his prayer, he felt a sudden gust of wind that blew through the open window and rustled the curtains. He looked up, surprised, but then brushed it off as just a coincidence.

But the next day, something strange happened. As he walked through the park, he noticed a small bird perched on a nearby tree branch. It looked straight at him and then flew down to land at his feet.

Charlie crouched to get a closer look and saw that the bird had a small piece of paper attached to its leg.

With trembling fingers, he carefully removed the paper and unfolded it. To his amazement, he saw that it was a handwritten note: "Charlie, you are loved. You are important. Keep going."

Tears streamed down Charlie's face as he looked around in disbelief. Had God really just sent him a message through a bird? He felt a sudden surge of hope and purpose that he had never felt before.

From that moment on, Charlie began to notice small signs and coincidences that seemed to guide him towards his purpose. He started volunteering at a homeless shelter and found joy in helping others. He reached out to old friends and family members whom he had lost touch with and found comfort in their love and support.

Although life was still tough at times, Charlie no longer felt alone. He knew that there was something greater than himself guiding him forward, and he embraced it with open arms.

Silence filled the room as Charlie waited for a response. He felt foolish talking to an entity that he wasn't even sure existed. But in that moment, he didn't care. He needed something, anything to hold onto.

As he sat there with his eyes closed, he felt a sudden chill wash over him. He opened his eyes and saw a figure standing in front of him. It was blurry at first but it slowly came into focus. It was a woman, with piercing blue eyes and a kind smile on her face.

"Hello Charlie," she said softly.

Charlie was frozen in place, unable to comprehend what was happening. Was this an apparition? A hallucination?

"I am here to help you," the woman said, walking towards him.

Charlie felt a wave of calm wash over him as she approached. He felt like he could trust her completely.

"What do you want from me?" he asked, his voice shaking.

"I want to show you your purpose," she replied, placing a hand on his shoulder.

And just like that, Charlie was transported into a vision. He saw himself helping others, bringing joy to those around him. He saw himself spreading kindness and compassion wherever he went.

When the vision faded away, Charlie was back in his room again, but he felt different. He felt like he had been given a purpose, like his life had meaning.

"Thank you," he whispered to the woman who had appeared before him.

And though she had disappeared, Charlie knew that she would be with him always, guiding him towards his purpose and helping him find his way in life.

Flashback: Chasity's death.

Charlie & Chasity pull up to his apartment building.

Suddenly a car speeds by being chased by police.

Gun shots are heard.

Charlie ducks down when he looks up Chasity isn't in the car.

He quickly gets out of the car to find Chasity lying dead on the side walk from a gunshot to the chest.

Charlie holding Chasity's head in his arms crying "I love you."

Cont.

Charlie looks up at the sky still crying and screams "Why, Why Chasity?"

The sound of his voice echoes through the empty streets as the police sirens fade away in the distance. Charlie could feel the shock setting in, numbing his mind and body. He couldn't believe Chasity was gone. The love of his life, taken away in a matter of seconds.

As he held her lifeless body, Charlie's heart raced with anger and pain. He knew he had to find whoever did this and make them pay. The streets were quiet, but Charlie had an idea where to start his search.

He gently laid Chasity down on the sidewalk and kissed her forehead. "I'll be back for you," he whispered before getting into his car.

Charlie drove through the city, searching for any signs of the car that had fled from the police. Hours passed, but he didn't give up hope. Suddenly, he saw a car that matched the description.

Charlie followed it through alleyways until it stopped in front of an abandoned warehouse. He parked his car and got out, his heart racing with adrenaline.

As he entered the warehouse, Charlie could hear voices coming from one of the back rooms. He carefully approached, peering through a gap in the door. What he saw made him furious.

A group of men were counting money and laughing as if they hadn't just taken a life. Charlie's hands clenched into fists as he stepped back, ready to take them down.

Without thinking twice, Charlie barged into the room and attacked them with all his might. Punches flew back and forth as he relentlessly fought to avenge Chasity's death.

As Charlie sat there holding Chasity's lifeless body, his mind raced back to how he had met her at a local coffee shop. She was sitting alone, reading a book, and he couldn't help but be drawn to her beauty. They started talking over lattes and before they knew it, hours had passed by like minutes.

Charlie felt a deep emptiness inside him, not only because he lost the love of his life, but also because he knew that he would never be able to hold her in his arms again. He decided to take matters into his own hands and started investigating the case, determined to find out what happened to her.

As he dug deeper, Charlie started uncovering some dirty secrets that were hidden beneath the surface. He found out that Chasity had been involved in some shady deals with some dangerous people and it was only a matter of time before something like this happened.

Despite all the danger, Charlie was determined to find justice for Chasity and make those responsible pay for what they had done. As he delved deeper into the investigation, Charlie realized that he was in way over his head, but he didn't care.

He was going to see this through until the end, even if it meant putting himself in harm's way. He looked down at Chasity one last time and whispered "I will find out who did this to you and make them pay." And with that, Charlie got up from the sidewalk, wiped away his tears, and walked towards the unknown dangers that lay ahead of him.

As he sat there holding her, Charlie couldn't help but feel numb. The love of his life was gone just like that. He didn't know how to process it all. He had never felt this kind of pain before.

Slowly, the sound of sirens filled the air as the police car pulled up. Charlie looked at Chasity one last time before standing up and turning towards the officers. They approached him with caution, unsure of what they were walking into.

Charlie's eyes were red from crying as he tried to explain what happened. The officers took down his statement and assured him they would do everything in their power to find the person responsible.

Days turned into weeks and weeks turned into months, but there was still no progress in the investigation. Charlie became consumed with grief and anger. He spent most of his days trying to piece together what happened and who could have done this.

One day, while Charlie was walking down the street, he saw a man who looked familiar. It was the same man who had been driving the car that day. All the pieces finally clicked into place, and Charlie knew he had found his culprit.

Without hesitation, Charlie lunged at the man, tackling him to the ground. Before anyone could intervene, Charlie was pounding on the man's face with all his might.

"You killed her! You took her away from me," Charlie screamed between blows.

It didn't take long for someone to call the police, and Charlie found himself being arrested for assault. But as he sat in his cell, he felt an odd sense of satisfaction knowing that he had gotten revenge for Chasity.

Charlie can feel his heart pounding in his chest as he cradles Chasity's lifeless body. He knows that all he ever wanted was for them to have a future together, but now those dreams are shattered forever. The anger and pain Charlie feels is unbearable. He can't understand how anyone could take the life of someone so innocent and pure.

As he looks up at the sky, numb with grief and despair, Charlie realizes that he has to keep moving forward. He has to make sure that the person who did this is brought to justice. Even if it means putting himself in harm's way, Charlie will stop at nothing to make sure that justice is served.

With tears streaming down his face, Charlie carries Chasity's body back to his car. He gently lays her down in the back seat and takes one last look at her beautiful face before closing the door. He knows that he has a long road ahead of him, but he also knows that Chasity would want him to be strong and fight for what is right.

As he drives away from the scene, Charlie can still hear the gunshots ringing in his ears. He clenches his fists in anger, vowing to never let anyone else suffer like Chasity did. With a newfound determination, Charlie sets out to find the person responsible for this senseless act of violence, no matter what it takes.

The road ahead is dark and dangerous, but Charlie knows that Chasity will always be with him, guiding him along the way. Together they will seek justice, and together they will find peace.

Hollywood & Chasity.

Chasity is standing in Charlie's living room watching him watch television.

Hollywood walks into the room.

Charlie gets up and walks into the kitchen.

Chasity: "I never got a chance to tell him I love him too."

Hollywood: "That sucks."

Chasity jumps and looks at Hollywood "You can hear me?"

Hollywood jumps and says "You can see me?"

They both pass out.

When Chasity woke up, she found herself lying on a soft bed in an unfamiliar room. It was dimly lit, and the walls were painted in a deep shade of blue. She groaned and rubbed her forehead, trying to recall what had happened.

Suddenly, the door creaked open, and Hollywood walked in holding a tray full of sandwiches and juice.

"Hey there, sleepyhead. You gave us quite a scare," he said, placing the tray on the bedside table.

Chasity sat up and frowned. "What happened? Where are we?"

Hollywood sighed and sat down next to her. "Charlie's house wasn't exactly what it seemed. He's part of a secret society that uses mind-control techniques to manipulate people's thoughts and feelings."

Chasity gasped as the memories flooded back. "That's why I couldn't confess my feelings to him," she whispered.

Hollywood nodded. "But we managed to escape just in time. And now we're safe here."

Chasity looked around the room and noticed there was only one bed. She blushed and shifted uncomfortably.

Hollywood noticed her discomfort and chuckled. "Relax. I'm not going to bite you."

Chasity laughed nervously and took a sip of juice. "So, what now? What do we do?"

"We find a way to expose Charlie's evil plans and stop him from causing harm to others," Hollywood replied firmly.

Chasity nodded in agreement. She felt a newfound sense of determination swelling inside her chest. She wasn't going to let anyone control her or manipulate her feelings ever again.

Chasity opens her eyes and finds herself in a dark room. The only light comes from a single flickering candle that illuminates the face of Hollywood lying next to her. She groans as she tries to get up, feeling a sharp pain in her head.

Hollywood stirs and rubs his eyes. "Are you okay?" he asks.

"I don't know," Chasity replies, holding her head. "Where are we?"

"I don't remember," Hollywood says, looking around the room. "But something tells me we're not alone."

Suddenly, they hear footsteps coming towards them. Chasity's heart races as she clutches onto Hollywood's arm.

A figure emerges from the shadows and steps into the candlelight. It's Charlie.

"What the hell is going on?" Chasity demands.

Charlie just stares at her with a blank expression before speaking in a monotone voice. "You both are going to do exactly what I say and nothing else. Understand?"

Chasity and Hollywood exchange worried glances before nodding slowly.

Charlie pulls out a gun from his back pocket and points it at them. "Good."

Chasity's mind races as she tries to figure out what Charlie wants. Is he going to kill them? Use them as hostages?

But then, she catches a glimpse of something behind Charlie. A book with strange symbols etched onto its cover sits on a table.

Her heart races as an idea forms in her mind.

Perhaps, if she can get her hands on that book, they can find a way out of this nightmare.

When Chasity and Hollywood woke up, they found themselves in a dimly lit room with no windows. The air was musty and thick with the scent of old books.

Chasity rubbed her eyes, trying to make sense of the situation. "Where are we?" she asked Hollywood.

"I have no idea," he replied, his eyes scanning the room.

Suddenly, a door on the far side of the room creaked open. A tall, lanky man with white hair and glasses stepped through the doorway. He wore a black suit and carried a cane, tapping it against the ground as he approached them.

"Welcome," he said, his voice slow and measured. "I am Professor Hargreaves. I have brought you here for a very specific purpose."

Chasity and Hollywood exchanged nervous glances but said nothing.

"I have read your books, both of you," the professor continued. "And I believe you have the potential to be great writers. But first, you must learn to let go of your inhibitions."

Hollywood narrowed his eyes. "What does that mean?"

The professor smiled wryly. "It means that in order to write truly great fiction, you must explore all aspects of life—the beautiful and the grotesque, the tender and the brutal."

Chasity felt her heart race as she realized what he was suggesting. "You mean we have to experience...everything?"

The professor nodded solemnly. "Yes. You must be willing to push past your boundaries and experience new things. Only then will you be able to write stories that truly resonate with your readers."

When Chasity regains consciousness, she is lying on a soft bed in a dark room. She sits up and looks around, trying to make sense of what happened. Suddenly, the door opens and Hollywood walks in.

"Thank god you're okay," he says, rushing over to her. "I thought you were dead."

Chasity looks at him, confused. "What happened? Where are we?"

"We're in my safe house," Hollywood explains. "After we both passed out, I brought us here to keep us safe."

"Safe from what?" Chasity asks.

Hollywood hesitates before answering. "There are people after us. Dangerous people. We need to lay low for a while."

Chasity's heart races as she realizes the gravity of the situation. She and Hollywood are in danger, and they have no idea who wants them dead or why.

As the days go by and they hide out in the safe house, Chasity begins to feel a deep connection with Hollywood. They spend long hours talking about everything from their childhoods to their hopes and dreams for the future. And one night, as they're sharing a bottle of wine by the fire, Hollywood takes her hand and says the words she's been longing to hear.

"Chasity, I love you."

She doesn't hesitate before responding. "I love you too."

From that moment on, they become inseparable. They work together to uncover the truth behind the danger that's been stalking them, relying on their wits and their love to keep each other safe.

Hollywood & Chasity 2.

Hollywood & Chasity sit up and look at each other.

Hollywood: "What are you looking at?"

Chasity: "Are you a ghost?"

Hollywood: "No, I'm what you could call an angel of sorts."

Chasity: "I was Charlie's girlfriend, my name was Chasity."

Hollywood: "Everyone calls me Hollywood, I was a comedian in a past life."

Chasity: "Why are you here?"

Hollywood: "I'm here because Charlie prayed and I was sent here to take him on a life journey and help him find happiness."

Chasity looked at Hollywood with a skeptical expression on her face. The idea of an angel coming to Earth to help Charlie find happiness seemed too good to be true.

"So, what's the catch?" she asked, crossing her arms over her chest.

Hollywood smiled and shook his head. "No catch. Charlie just needed some guidance, and I'm here to offer it."

Chasity hesitated for a moment before asking, "And what about me? Do I get to come along on this life journey?"

Hollywood looked at her thoughtfully for a moment before nodding. "Of course. Charlie cared about you deeply, and I believe he would have wanted you to be a part of this journey as well."

Chasity felt a sense of relief wash over her. She had been feeling lost and alone since Charlie's passing, and the idea of embarking on a new adventure with Hollywood felt like exactly what she needed.

"Okay," she said softly. "I'm ready."

Hollywood stood up from the couch and held out a hand to Chasity. "Let's go then."

Chasity stared at Hollywood in disbelief. She had never believed in angels or ghosts, but seeing Hollywood's ethereal presence right in front of her was undeniable.

"So, you're here to take Charlie on a life journey?" Chasity asked, still incredulous.

Hollywood nodded. "Yes, that's right. Charlie was lost and he needed guidance. And I'm here to give him that."

Chasity leaned back in her chair, still trying to process everything that was happening. "But why Charlie? Why did he need your help?"

Hollywood let out a deep sigh. "Charlie was going through a particularly rough patch in his life. He was feeling lost and alone, and he didn't know where to turn. But I saw something in him that others didn't see - a spark, a potential for greatness."

Chasity frowned. "Greatness? Charlie was just a small town boy with big dreams. He wanted to make it as a musician, but he never did."

Hollywood smiled softly. "Ah, but that's where you're wrong, my dear. Charlie did make it - just not in the way that he wanted to."

Chasity raised an eyebrow. "What do you mean?"

Hollywood leaned forward, his eyes glittering with an otherworldly light. "Charlie's music touched people's souls. It made them feel things that they never knew they could feel. And even though he never became a famous musician, his music will live on forever."

Chasity's eyes widened in surprise as she listened to Hollywood's explanation. She had always believed in the existence of angels, but she had never actually met one before.

"So, you're here to help Charlie find happiness?" Chasity asked, looking at Hollywood expectantly.

"Yes," Hollywood replied, nodding his head. "Charlie has been going through a lot lately and he needs guidance. That's where I come in."

Chasity thought about this for a moment before speaking again. "What kind of journey are you taking him on?"

Hollywood smiled knowingly. "It's a journey of self-discovery," he said. "Charlie needs to learn who he truly is and what he truly wants out of life. Only then can he find true happiness."

Chasity felt a warm feeling spread throughout her body as she listened to Hollywood speak. She knew that Charlie had been struggling with depression for a while now, and maybe this was just what he needed to finally find some peace.

"I hope you can help him," she said quietly.

Hollywood looked at her kindly. "I will do everything in my power to help him," he said. "But I could also use your help."

"My help?" Chasity asked, surprised.

"Yes," Hollywood replied. "You were Charlie's girlfriend and you know him better than anyone else. You can help me guide him on this journey."

A sense of purpose filled Chasity as she nodded her head in agreement. She was ready and willing to do whatever it took to help Charlie find happiness once again.

Chasity's eyes widened in surprise. "Charlie prayed for help?" she asked, incredulous.

Hollywood nodded solemnly. "He did. And now it's my job to guide him. But I can't do it alone."

Chasity frowned, unsure of what to do. "What can I do to help?"

Hollywood smiled, a mischievous gleam in his eye. "Well, for starters, we need to shake Charlie out of his funk. Get him out of the house. Maybe a night out on the town?"

Chasity nodded eagerly, feeling a spark of excitement in her chest. She missed Charlie terribly, and if there was any chance to bring him back to his old self, she was willing to do whatever it took.

Together, Hollywood and Chasity concocted a plan to take Charlie out for a night on the town. They dressed him up in his finest suit and dragged him to a local jazz club.

At first, Charlie was hesitant and withdrawn, but as the night wore on, he began to let loose. Chasity watched in amazement as the man she loved began to laugh and dance once again.

As the night came to a close and they headed back home, Hollywood turned to Chasity with a knowing gleam in his eye. "We did good tonight," he said with a smirk.

Chasity blushed, feeling an unfamiliar heat rise in her cheeks. As much as she was drawn to Charlie's old self, she couldn't deny the fluttering feeling in her stomach whenever Hollywood was near.

Bathroom.

Charlie steps out of the shower and sees Hollywood standing in the doorway and screams and grabs the towel.

Hollywood: "Damn, I see why you're depressed if I had a dick that small I would be depressed too."

Charlie: "What, who are you?"

Hollywood: "I'm Hollywood, I was sent here to help you find your path in life and hopefully help you find happiness."

Charlie: "You're an angel."

Hollywood: "Yes, by the way sorry about Chasity, she was kind of hot."

Charlie: "Thanks."

Hollywood stepped forward and Charlie could feel the heat emanating from his body. He was tall and muscular with chiseled features that made Charlie's heart skip a beat. Hollywood reached out and ran his finger down Charlie's chest, making him shiver.

"So, Charlie, what do you want in life?" Hollywood asked, his voice low and seductive.

Charlie gulped, feeling a sudden surge of desire. He had never felt this way before, but he knew he wanted this man. "I... I'm not sure," he stammered.

Hollywood chuckled and leaned in closer. "Don't worry, I'll help you figure it out."

He pressed his lips against Charlie's mouth, sending sparks shooting through Charlie's body. Charlie kissed him back eagerly, feeling like he'd found something he'd been missing his whole life.

The two of them stumbled back toward the bed, their mouths locked together as Hollywood peeled off Charlie's towel. They fell onto the mattress, writhing together in a frenzy of desire.

For the first time in a long time, Charlie felt happy. With Hollywood by his side, he knew that he could face whatever life threw at him and come out on top.

Hollywood leans against the bathroom doorway, still eyeing Charlie up and down. Charlie tries to cover himself up with the towel, but Hollywood just chuckles.

Hollywood: "Don't worry about that towel, baby. I've seen it all before."

Charlie feels a sudden tingle in his stomach as Hollywood takes slow steps towards him, placing gentle hands on Charlie's waist. Hollywood leans in close and whispers in Charlie's ear.

Hollywood: "Let me help you find happiness, Charlie. Let me show you true pleasure."

Charlie hesitates for a moment, but the feeling of Hollywood's hands on his skin is too much to resist. As they kiss passionately, Charlie forgets about his depression and his past life, consumed by the heat of the moment.

In the days that follow, Hollywood becomes Charlie's constant companion, introducing him to a world of pleasure and excitement beyond anything he could have imagined. Together, they explore the city at night and indulge in their wildest desires.

But as their relationship deepens, Hollywood's true nature is revealed. He is not an angel but a demon sent to lead Charlie down a path of destruction and damnation. And soon enough, Charlie finds himself caught up in a world of sin and violence, unable to escape the clutches of Hollywood and his dark influence.

Hollywood sat down on the edge of Charlie's bed. He crossed his ankles and rested his hands on his bare knees, gazing at Charlie through dark lashes.

"So, what brings you to me?" Charlie asked, wrapping the towel firmly around his waist.

Hollywood raised an eyebrow and tilted his head to the side. "Isn't it obvious? Your depression, your lack of direction in life."

Charlie sighed heavily and ran a hand through his wet hair. "Yeah, I guess you're right," he admitted.

Hollywood smiled softly and leaned closer to Charlie. "I'm here to show you the way, to help you find your true passion in life," he whispered.

Charlie felt a shiver run down his spine as Hollywood's breath tickled his ear. He swallowed hard and tried to ignore the sudden stirring in his groin.

"What do I have to do?" he asked, his voice barely above a whisper.

Hollywood chuckled and ran a finger down Charlie's chest. "Just relax, let me take care of everything," he murmured.

And with that, Hollywood leaned in and captured Charlie's lips in a heated kiss. Charlie moaned as he melted into the embrace, his towel forgotten as it slipped off and pooled at his feet.

As Hollywood deepened the kiss, Charlie felt something inside him shift. Was this what he had been missing all along? The touch of someone who understood him, who could guide him towards happiness?

He didn't know where this would lead, but for now he was content to lose himself in Hollywood's embrace and let him lead the way.

Hollywood steps forward and offers Charlie a hand to shake.

Hollywood: "Let's get dressed and we can go grab a drink and talk more about your life."

Charlie nods in agreement and walks into his room to start getting dressed. As he rummages through his closet, trying to find something decent to wear, Hollywood continues to speak.

Hollywood: "So, Charlie, tell me more about yourself. What do you like to do? What are your interests?"

Charlie thinks for a moment before answering.

Charlie: "Honestly, I don't know. Depression has sort of taken over my life lately. I used to be interested in a lot of things but now I just don't care anymore."

Hollywood nods understandingly.

Hollywood: "Depression is a tough battle, but I'm here to help you fight it. Maybe we can explore some new hobbies together and you'll find something that sparks your interest once again."

Charlie smiles at the thought and finishes getting dressed.

They head out to a nearby bar and sit down at a booth with drinks in hand.

Hollywood: "So, what do you say we try something new tonight? Let's go dancing!"

Charlie hesitates for a moment but ultimately agrees, wanting to break out of his shell and try something new.

On the dance floor, Hollywood shows off some moves that Charlie has never seen before. He watches in awe as Hollywood dances flawlessly, completely losing himself in the music.

As they dance together, Charlie begins to feel a sense of joy he hasn't felt in a long time. With each step he feels more confident and free.

What now?

Charlie: "So, what are you going to do?"

Hollywood: "Well I'm gonna take you on a trip through time."

Charlie: "I hope it's not some cheesy type deal."

Hollywood: "Don't worry it'll be fun."

Chasity looks at Hollywood and says "I know you're up to something."

Hollywood nods.

Charlie: "Ok cool."

Hollywood's eyes glinted with excitement as he led Charlie and Chasity to his time machine, which was hidden behind a curtain in his cramped apartment. As they entered the dimly-lit room, Hollywood flipped a switch and a blinding light enveloped them.

When the light abated, they found themselves in what appeared to be a medieval village. The air smelled of smoke and rotting food, and the ground was muddy and treacherous. Charlie felt a wave of panic wash over him.

"What the hell is going on?" he demanded.

Hollywood grinned mischievously. "Relax, we're in 14th century England. I wanted to show you guys what it was like to live during the Black Death."

Chasity's face paled at the mention of the plague, but Hollywood ushered them through the village without pause. As they passed by hovels made of sticks and mud, villagers recoiled from them in fear.

Charlie couldn't believe how differently people lived back then. Disease seemed rampant, and there was no modern medicine or technology to save them. It was chilling to think about.

Just as they were about to leave the village, a young woman caught Charlie's attention. She was covered in sores and her breathing was ragged. She looked like she was in incredible pain.

"Who is she?" Charlie asked.

Hollywood hesitated for a moment before answering. "Her name is Anna, she's dying of the plague."

Charlie felt an overwhelming urge to help her in some way - to ease her suffering, even if just a little.

Hollywood grabs Charlie's hand and leads him out of the room, while Chasity follows closely behind. They walk down a narrow hallway, and as they approach a door at the end of it, Hollywood turns to them with a sly smile on his face.

"Are you ready for this?" he asks.

Charlie nods eagerly, and Chasity shoots Hollywood a look of suspicion. He opens the door and motions for them to follow him inside.

What they see takes their breath away. They are standing in a dimly lit room, filled with an array of strange and mysterious objects. There are shelves lining every wall, and each one is packed with artifacts from different eras in history.

Hollywood gestures grandly to the room. "Welcome to my time machine."

Chasity scoffs. "You can't be serious. This is all just a bunch of junk."

But Hollywood ignores her, instead turning to Charlie with an excited glint in his eye. "So, where do you want to go first?"

Charlie looks around at all the strange objects in awe. "I don't know, maybe Ancient Greece?"

Hollywood claps his hands together. "Excellent choice! Hold on tight."

With that, he pulls a lever on one of the machines in the room, and suddenly everything around them blurs into a dizzying mess of colors and shapes.

When they finally come to a stop, they find themselves standing in front of the Parthenon in Athens. The sun is setting over the city, casting a warm glow over everything around them.

As Hollywood led Charlie and Chasity down the dark alley, he could feel their excitement. He had promised to take them on a trip through time, and he planned to deliver.

He stopped at a nondescript door and knocked twice. A few moments later, it opened, revealing a dimly lit room.

"Welcome to my time machine," Hollywood said with a grin.

Charlie and Chasity looked at each other in amazement as they stepped inside, marveling at the blinking lights and whirring gears that filled the room.

"Just sit back and enjoy the ride," Hollywood said as he flicked a switch, and the room began to shake.

As they traveled through time, Charlie and Chasity saw incredible sights. They watched as knights jousted on horseback, saw pirates on the high seas, and witnessed the birth of the steam engine.

But as they arrived in the roaring twenties, something strange happened. Hollywood disappeared, leaving Charlie and Chasity alone in a crowded speakeasy.

Suddenly, the lights went out, and a hush fell over the crowd. A voice spoke from the darkness.

"I've been waiting for you," it said.

Charlie and Chasity looked at each other nervously as they realized they were no longer in control of their journey through time.

Hollywood proceeded to pull out a strange device from his pocket. He pressed a few buttons and suddenly, the air around them began to shimmer. Charlie's eyes widened as he felt his body being pulled forward, as if through time and space.

The next thing he knew, they were standing in what looked like an old-fashioned saloon. The smell of whiskey and tobacco was thick in the air, and the sound of piano music filled the room. Charlie couldn't believe his eyes - had they really traveled back in time?

As he looked around, he realized that Hollywood had disappeared. Suddenly, a woman caught his eye. She was beautiful, with long dark hair and piercing green eyes that seemed to look right through him.

"Hey there," she said, giving him a flirty smile. "What brings a handsome stranger like you to this part of town?"

Charlie opened his mouth to respond when the doors to the saloon suddenly burst open. A group of rough-looking men carrying guns marched in, their faces twisted into snarls.

It was only then that Charlie realized the gravity of their situation. They were stuck in a time before modern conveniences and laws.

He looked around frantically for Hollywood or even Chasity but saw no signs of either of them. It was up to him now to figure out how to get them out of this mess.

Your first bottle.

Hollywood & Charlie are in Charlie's parent's house.

Charlie's mom is holding baby Charlie.

Charlie: "What do we have here?"

Hollywood: "Your first bottle of ..."

Charlie picks up a bottle of milk and starts drinking it.

Hollywood: "What are you doing?"

Charlie: "I like milk."

Hollywood: "You picked up the wrong bottle, that's horse cum."

Charlie spits it out.

Chasity laughs and says "That's horse cum."

Charlie: "What is it?"

Hollywood: "It's horse cum."

Charlie: "Why do you horses cum?"

Hollywood: "We have sex, and cum is how we reproduce."

Hollywood goes out to the barn and pours another cup of cum into a bottle.

He goes back in.

Hollywood: "Here you go."

Charlie hits his cup against Hollywood's.

They look at each other and drink the cum together. They both spit it out onto the ground.

Hollywood: "Fuck. I mean, I know horse cum tastes like crap but I didn't know it would taste that bad!"

Chasity: "Aww yeah, fuckin hick. If you gotta stick ya dick in a horse, just drink more whiskey before you fuck the damn thing huh?! You heard your momma huh?! You heard her Chasity?! Fuckin hick! Just drinking whiskey to kill his taste buds, man..."

Charlie wipes his mouth with the back of his hand.

Charlie: "Tastes like tits though... Like... Like the actual tits on a girl..."

Chasity laughs really loudly while Charlie is saying this as he is thinking of what it would be like eating some tits one day. Hollywood and Charlie are getting a little drunk already but Chasity is already well on her way.

Charlie: "Funny!"

Charlie looks at his mom.

Charity: "You're gonna be handsome one day just like yer daddy."

Hollywood's sister: "What about me? I had him when I was 14, I look like a 45 year old grandma. How will I have fun with no fun body? Ha ha ha ha ."

Charity: "Don't worry honey, a lot of people will have that same problem, they call it a charity for celebs and rich people ."

Hollywood: "Oh please, shut up and be cool."

Charlie: "Oh."

Hollywood: "She said don't you ever drink out of that bottle again."

While having a bubble bath.

Chasity: "It smells good."

Charlie: "Yeah, it smells like candy land in here."

While playing with a toy guitar.

Charlie: "Shit ride? I cry tears of joy... Because fucking shit ride! Shit, ride! Now saying shit doesn't matter right? But if I was saying something else, I would get in trouble because it isn't appropriate, isn't that the same for you?"

Charlie: "When we first got married, we were dating for 3 and a half years; dating on different terms... girlfriend/boyfriend for 3 years and then husband/wife for another 12 months... so I know when you sleep with somebody three times – maybe not 3 times... it might take awhile. Like everybody is different, right? So maybe their libido takes awhile to kick in. Like some people just can't do it till they been going out for seven months or eight months, 11 months or this was the first time they see ass – before they see ass, their libido is nonexistent because they don't understand what they're missing. But I know that there are other girls that can get with anybody and act like a prostitute the first time seeing [them]. Just so she can get opened up or something...

Charlie: "Oh. What do I look like?"

Chasity: "You have a face like a horse."

Charlie looks in the mirror at his face and he thinks it looks like a horse.

Charlie is on the phone with Hollywood.

Charlie says "From now on I'm going to be an actor, a star!"

Hollywood: "What?! You're going to be an actor? Like Lincoln?"

Charlie: "Like Lincoln."

Hollywood: "Who?"

Chasity: "It's okay, he probably just made him say that."

Hollywood: "What are you doing? You can't become an actor!"

Charlie: "I know, that's why I called to threaten you so you help me become an actor. I'm gonna tell everyone you gave me millions of dollars. I think you owe me a lot of money. Tell him Chasity."

Chasity says in agreement.

Hollywood: "That was years ago, we worked together and drank at every bar and diner around ... Why would I give you all that money for just drinking?"

Charlie: "I don't know why but I was pretty drunk back then. All I remember is a lot of sex with assholes and hookahs and ... Hold on Hollywood, someone just opened my briefcase...oh! Oh! It was llamas! Why did you make so...."

Your first date.

Hollywood & Charlie are in the restaurant where Charlie had his first date.

Charlie: "What are we doing here?"

Hollywood: "This is where you had your first date."

Charlie: "Oh yeah."

Hollywood: "Do you remember what you ate?"

Charlie: "No."

Cut to the chef picking up a jar that says "Goat balls" on the label.

Hollywood: "You ate goat balls."

Charlie: "Oh sick." Pukes.

Chasity: "What kind of sick freak cooks goat balls?"

Hollywood and Charlie turn around to see Chasity, a stunning young woman with piercing blue eyes and long blonde hair walking towards them. She had a disgusted expression on her face as she looked at the jar in the chef's hand.

Hollywood: "I think we should ask the chef that question."

Chasity: "I'm sorry, I didn't mean to interrupt. My name is Chasity. I couldn't help but overhear your conversation."

Charlie: "It's okay. I'm Charlie, and this is Hollywood."

Hollywood: "Nice to meet you, Chasity."

Chasity: "You guys seem like you're on a date. Mind if I join you?"

Charlie and Hollywood look at each other for a moment before nodding in agreement.

As they sit down, Chasity orders a glass of red wine, and they all start chatting about their favorite movies and TV shows. They find out that they have a lot in common and end up laughing over shared jokes.

As the night draws to a close, Charlie walks Chasity to her car and leans in for a kiss. She responds eagerly, and soon they are passionately making out.

Hollywood discreetly slips away, happy for his friend who seemed to have finally found someone he truly connected with.

Hollywood shrugged. "I mean, apparently this restaurant does."

Charlie wiped his mouth with a napkin. "Can we please change the subject? I'm not feeling too well."

Chasity took a seat next to Charlie and put her hand on his back. "Are you okay?"

He nodded. "Yeah, I'll be fine. Just need a minute."

Hollywood leaned forward in his chair, his eyes scanning the room. "Something doesn't feel right."

Chasity furrowed her brows. "What do you mean?"

"I don't know." Hollywood stood up, his eyes darting around the room. "I just have a bad feeling."

As he spoke, the door to the restaurant burst open and several men entered, all wearing dark clothing and carrying guns.

"Everyone get down!" one of them shouted.

Charlie pushed Chasity under the table and crawled in after her. Hollywood quickly followed suit.

They huddled together under the table as gunshots rang out throughout the restaurant. Charlie could hear people screaming and glass shattering.

What felt like an eternity passed before the gunfire ceased. Charlie slowly lifted the tablecloth and peeked out from underneath.

The restaurant was in shambles, tables overturned and broken glass littering the floor. The men who had entered earlier had fled.

Charlie looked over at Chasity and Hollywood. They were both unharmed but visibly shaken.

"What just happened?" Chasity asked, her voice trembling.

"I don't know," Charlie said, standing up from under the table. "But we need to get out of here."

As Charlie tried to compose himself, Chasity walked over to their table. Hollywood flashed her a charming smile and pulled out a chair for her.

"It's an acquired taste," the chef said as he walked over with a menu. "But don't worry, we have plenty of other options."

Chasity scanned the menu before deciding on a salad. As she put down her menu, her eyes locked onto Hollywood's.

"So what brings you two here?" she asked.

Hollywood leaned back in his chair and took a sip of water. "We're actually working on a project together," he said.

Charlie watched as Chasity's eyes widened with interest. He knew Hollywood was always good at spinning stories to attract attention.

"That sounds exciting," Chasity said. "What kind of project?"

Before Hollywood could answer, the lights in the restaurant flickered and then went out completely. Charlie heard screams from other diners as they stumbled around trying to find their way out.

Someone bumped into Charlie's chair, sending him sprawling onto the ground. He felt a pair of hands grab him and help him up.

"Charlie, are you okay?" It was Chasity's voice.

The emergency lights flickered on, casting a dim red glow over the restaurant. Charlie looked up to see Hollywood standing in front of them, his face blank.

"We need to get out of here," Hollywood said. "Now."

As Chasity's voice boomed, Hollywood quickly turned around, surprised to see his ex-girlfriend standing behind him, along with her friends. Chasity had always been the queen of drama, and seeing her here made Hollywood anxious.

Ignoring her comment, he turned back to Charlie, "You okay man?" But before Charlie could answer, Chasity's friend interrupted.

"Excuse me," she said pointing at the dish in front of them. "But what the hell is this?"

Hollywood chuckled, "Goat balls. You know, they're actually quite tasty."

Chasity rolled her eyes, "Of course you would like that shit."

Ignoring her comment once more, Hollywood turned to the chef and ordered a round of drinks for everyone at the table.

As they waited for their drinks, Chasity couldn't help but notice the chemistry between Hollywood and one of his new friends at the table. Her jealousy and anger were starting to build up inside.

"Who's your friend?" she asked pointedly.

Hollywood introduced her as Amber. And as he did, he noticed Chasity's gaze lingering a little too long on his new companion. He could sense the jealousy radiating off her in waves.

After a few more drinks and some conversations filled with awkward silences and forced small talk, Hollywood decided it was time to leave.

As they walked out of the restaurant, Charlie leaned over to Hollywood and whispered, "Thanks for taking me here man. I owe you one."

Hollywood smiled back at him. "Anytime bro."

Your first car.

Hollywood & Charlie are in Charlie's first car.

The car is so slow everything passes them.

Charlie looks out and a baby crawls by and gives him the finger "My first car."

Hollywood: "This car is a piece of shit."

Charlie looks out the window and a turtle passes him and gives him the finger.

Hollywood: "I heard Tara Reid and Lindsay Lohan lost their virginity in the back seat."

Charlie: "That explains why it was free."

Chasity laughs.

Hollywood: "That also explains why the trunk is full of used condoms and tickets to acting classes."

Charlie: "They should have used the tickets to acting classes instead of the condoms."

As they continued down the road, the car's engine began to sputter. Hollywood and Charlie shared a worried look before the vehicle came to a complete stop. Charlie cursed under his breath and tried to restart the car, but it wouldn't budge.

Just as Charlie was about to give up, a sleek black car pulled up behind them. The tinted window rolled down slowly, revealing a gorgeous woman with bright red lipstick and an expensive-looking outfit.

"Having car trouble?" she asked, her voice smooth as honey.

Charlie gulped nervously and nodded. Hollywood shot him a questioning look, but Charlie just shrugged in response.

The woman stepped out of her car and strutted over to them, her heels clicking against the pavement. "I might be able to help," she said coyly, running a hand down Charlie's chest.

He swallowed hard and tried not to stumble over his words. "Th-thank you, miss. I don't know what we'd do without your help."

The woman just smirked and walked over to the engine. Within moments, she had identified the problem and fixed it with ease.

Charlie was more grateful than ever as he climbed back into his car, feeling lucky to have encountered such a kind stranger. As he started the engine, he couldn't help but wonder who she was and why she had helped them so willingly.

But before they could dwell on it any longer, the woman hopped back into her own car and sped off down the road. Charlie watched her go in awe before turning back to Hollywood with a grin on his face.

As they continued to drive, the car sputtered and coughed, threatening to break down at any moment. Charlie's face was flushed with embarrassment as pedestrians continued to pass them with ease. Hollywood rolled down the window and shouted at the next person who passed by.

Hollywood: "Hey, did you see that? We're driving a damn lawn mower!"

The person turned around and flipped them off, causing Hollywood to burst into laughter. Charlie felt his frustration growing with every passing moment. Suddenly, the car shuddered and came to a stop in the middle of the road.

Charlie: "Oh no, what now?"

Hollywood got out of the car and kicked the tire in frustration.

Hollywood: "This is just great. Now we're stranded in this piece of junk!"

Charlie opened the glove box and found a map of the city.

Charlie: "I think there's a mechanic shop a few blocks from here. We can push it there."

Chasity got out of the car and began pushing, followed by Hollywood and Charlie. They made their way through the busy streets, dodging angry drivers honking their horns. Finally, they arrived at the mechanic shop and pushed the car inside.

Mechanic: "What seems to be the problem?"

Charlie: "I don't know. It just stopped working."

The mechanic inspected the car and shook his head.

Mechanic: "You're lucky you made it this far. This car is a death trap."

Hollywood chuckled.

Hollywood: "Tell us something we don't know."

As they drive along the deserted road, Hollywood checks his phone and sees a text from their drug dealer, Oscar. He tells them that the shipment is ready and they can pick it up any time they like.

Hollywood turns to Charlie, excitement etched on his face. "Hey man, wanna go pick up our stuff? We can make a quick stop and get high before heading to the party."

Charlie hesitates for a moment but then agrees. The urge for some drugs is too strong to resist. Plus, he has always been curious about what it feels like to get high.

As they drive towards the dealer's hideout, Hollywood hands Charlie a joint. "Just take small puffs", he says with a grin.

Charlie inhales the smoke and feels it fill his lungs. A warm sensation spreads throughout his body as he exhales. The music on the radio starts to sound different, better. His vision gets a little blurry but he doesn't mind.

As they approach Oscar's place, they see him standing outside with a group of people. Hollywood parks the car and they both step out, walking towards him.

Oscar greets them with a smile and hands them a small black package. "You boys have fun tonight", he says with a wink.

Excitedly, they head back to the car and open up the package. Inside are some pills and powder wrapped in plastic bags.

Hollywood grins at Charlie. "It's party time!", he exclaims as he pops a pill into his mouth.

As they drove on, the rickety car made strange noises and Charlie was worried it would break down at any moment. Just as he thought this, smoke started pouring out from under the hood.

"Shit, I think the car's overheating," Charlie said nervously.

Hollywood rolled his eyes and muttered, "No shit, Sherlock."

Chasity looked around nervously, trying to assess their surroundings. They were in a deserted area with no sign of civilization for miles around.

Just as they thought things couldn't get any worse, they heard a loud pop and felt the car lurch forward before finally coming to a stop.

"Well, that's just perfect," Hollywood grumbled. "Looks like we'll have to walk from here."

Charlie and Chasity sighed resignedly and got out of the car. As they walked down the empty road, Charlie couldn't help but feel like he was in some sort of horror movie - stranded in the middle of nowhere with no way out.

But then he saw something up ahead - a small cabin nestled among the trees. Without thinking, he started running towards it.

"Charlie, wait up!" Chasity called after him.

But Charlie kept running until he reached the cabin door and knocked frantically.

The door opened and a beautiful woman appeared, looking at Charlie with confusion.

"Can we use your phone?" Charlie gasped.

The woman hesitated for a moment before nodding and allowing them inside. As they waited for help to arrive, Charlie couldn't help but feel grateful for his crappy old car that had led them to this chance encounter.

Your first lady man.

Hollywood & Charlie are in Charlie's apartment.

Charlie: "What are we doing here?"

Hollywood: "This is the first time you bring home a chick..."

Charlie: "Alright."

Hollywood: "She has a dick."

Chasity laughs.

Charlie: "Damn it."

Hollywood, Charlie, and Chasity were all left in an awkward silence. Charlie didn't know what to say, while Hollywood tried to break the tension.

"So, uh...what do you guys want to do?" Hollywood suggested.

Chasity spoke up. "I don't know about you guys, but I'm down for whatever." She grinned at them both.

Charlie couldn't help but feel a little betrayed. He had been flirting with Chasity all night, and not once did she mention that she was transgender. Normally, he wouldn't mind, but he felt like she should have been more upfront about it.

Hollywood sensed his friend's discomfort and said, "Hey man, it's cool. Let's just chill and have a good time."

With that, they all settled on the couch and began watching a movie. Charlie couldn't concentrate on the film though - his mind kept wandering back to Chasity's revelation.

After awhile, Chasity got up to use the restroom. Hollywood immediately turned to Charlie and said, "Dude, you gotta relax. It's not that big of a deal."

Charlie shook his head. "It's just...I don't know how I feel about it. I mean, she's still hot and everything...but it's just weird."

Hollywood sighed. "Look man, if you're not into her anymore, that's fine. But don't be an asshole about it."

Charlie nodded in agreement. When Chasity returned to the couch, they all sat in silence for a few more minutes before she stood up to leave.

"It was nice meeting you guys,"

Charlie couldn't believe it. He had finally worked up the courage to bring a woman home, and now he found out she was actually a he. He struggled to compose himself as Chasity continued to laugh.

Hollywood seemed to find the whole situation amusing too, but Charlie couldn't see the humor in it. He had always considered himself to be open-minded, but this was too much for him.

As he tried to figure out what to do next, Chasity walked over to him and put a hand on his shoulder.

"Don't worry about it," she said, her voice low and sultry. "I understand if you're not into that kind of thing."

Charlie looked up at her and saw the sincerity in her eyes. Despite the shock of finding out her true gender, he couldn't help but feel drawn to her. She was beautiful and confident, and there was something about her that made him want to know more.

He took a deep breath and decided to go with the flow. After all, he had brought her home for a reason.

"Let's just see where the night takes us," he said with a small smile.

Chasity grinned back at him, and Hollywood rolled his eyes.

"Well, I'll leave you two lovebirds alone," he said as he headed for the door. "Just remember to use protection."

Charlie ignored his friend's snarky comment as Chasity led him to the bedroom. He knew this wasn't going to be a typical night, but for some reason, he was excited about what lay ahead.

Chasity: "Is that a problem?" She raises an eyebrow, her hands on her hips. Hollywood grins, his eyes scanning Chasity's body appreciatively.

Hollywood: "Not for me."

Charlie looks uncomfortable, his eyes flickering between Hollywood and Chasity.

Charlie: "I don't know if I'm into that."

Chasity shrugs, a small smile playing on her lips.

Chasity: "That's okay. Not everyone is."

Hollywood steps closer to Chasity, his hand reaching out to brush against the curve of her hip.

Hollywood: "But maybe you can convince him otherwise. Show him what he's been missing."

Charlie watches as Hollywood leans in, his lips brushing against Chasity's neck. He feels a surge of jealousy mixed with arousal.

Charlie: "Okay...I'll give it a try."

Chasity turns towards him, her eyes locking with his.

Chasity: "Just relax and let me show you how good it can feel."

As she speaks, she runs her hand down Charlie's chest before slowly dropping to her knees in front of him. Charlie watches as she unzips his pants and takes him in her mouth. He groans, feeling himself get harder with each passing second.

Meanwhile, Hollywood moves behind Chasity, his hands roaming over her hips and ass. They move together as a team, pleasuring Charlie in ways he never thought possible.

As Charlie processed what Hollywood had just said, his heart sank with the realization that everything he had hoped for was about to be shattered. He had met Chasity at a bar the previous night and she seemed like the perfect girl for him. They had hit it off immediately, talking and laughing as if they had known each other their entire lives.

Now, as he looked at her with new eyes, all he could think about was the fact that her body didn't match the one he had been expecting. Hollywood's words echoed in his mind over and over again, and he couldn't believe this was happening.

Chasity, on the other hand, seemed perfectly calm - almost as if she had been waiting for this moment to happen. She looked at Charlie with a knowing smile on her face and spoke softly.

"I understand if this is too much for you," she said. "But I want you to know that I'm still the same person you met last night. My body doesn't define who I am."

Charlie didn't know what to say. He felt like he had been deceived, but at the same time, he couldn't deny the attraction he still felt towards Chasity. Her words rang true to him, and he realized that she was right - her body didn't define her.

With a deep breath, Charlie looked at Chasity and took her hand in his. "I'm sorry for my reaction earlier," he said. "I just didn't expect this."

Chasity smiled at him again, grateful for his understanding. "Thank you," she said. "I appreciate it."

Your first walk in.

Hollywood & Charlie are in Charlie's parent's bedroom.

Charlie: "What are we doing here?"

Hollywood: "This is the first time you walk in on your parents having sex."

Charlie: "Oh shit."

Hollywood: "And you find out your dad likes it up the ass."

Charlie: "What the fuck?" Pukes.

Chasity: "Oh my god." Laughs.

Hollywood: "Well, he's also kind of loose around the waistline."

Charlie scans the room. Jr. watches him from the corner.

Charlie: "Dad! What the fuck?" Scared. What is his father's penis going to do?

Dave: "Come here, son. Let Daddy show you how it's done."

Charlie: "No! No! No! Chasity!" He runs out of the room and down the stairs. Dave dives after him, lettuce hanging out of his ass is slapping against his thighs and balls.

Hollywood: "Or maybe you've got mommy issues and your getting a blowjob from your brother is what you always wanted but too afraid to ask for it so you say no and run off because you know deep inside if he accepted what you really wanted he would leave you, but deep down inside if he said no then you would be so angry that you'd end up getting killed by yourself because deep down inside all you wanted was to get it in your butt like dad."

Charlie: "Fuck, man. That makes sense to me, Hollywood. It feels right coming from you. Because I am a lonely lonely man who doesn't know what is going on with my life. I don't like how things are right now with me and Sophie so maybe we need to break up because I'm too scared to let her love me for who I am, which is a hung stud that will give her whatever she needs whenever she needs it.

"That ain't funny. Hollywood was here at the time."

41

Charlie: "That's raunchy as fuck. Hollywood, what the fuck? I'm surprised you could even mention that without puking."

Charlie: "Yeah, no, I remember that though. That was retarded, and before Chasity, let me tell you, she would not have found that shi-, she would not have thought that was funny. She may have thought it was gross and nasty, but it wouldn't have been funny to her, whereas now..."

Chasity: "No no no no, it was funny when it happened to me. It's just how you tell it."

Charlie: "Jason told you a different way to tell the story and it made you laugh. Or not laugh because you know what happened, kind of laughing at me because I didn't know what happened and telling me your version of the ricochet story was hilarious, but definitely played upon my ignorance. But that joke right there, ahahhaaha haha haha haha hahahahhahahaha! Because I love him, Hollywood can do no wrong.

Charlie: "Really? Go on..."

Chasity: "I hear what you're saying. What Charlie is saying is that Hollywood was as miserable as he ever has been in his life that day at work. And then he just repressed the memory so much that even when he talked to Jason and told this story so differently than what actually happened.

Rico: "You guys are so funny."

Rocky: "I have to say you've got a great ass but I don't like to ride the wild bronco when it comes to dicks. I like that Charlie guy. He likes dicks. Over here he's doing all of this crazy shit with dicks in his mouth and having three guys at once drilling him or something. What a little slut. Maybe we should just fuck around. And see who gets off quick from the excitement of all the other ramming dicks in the air?"

Chasity: "Maybe we should have Charlie and Jekyll over in a threesome while Roxie watches?"

Rico: "What if Roxie is on top of me while Charlie is on top of you while Jekyll is giving me head? Oh hey, have you seen that pink vibrating dick up near the front counter?"

Rocky: "Maybe we should get hot and sweaty and whoop it up with some fun foreplay sex stuff. And then let's do the girls first, then we can watch each other blow our loads all over Charlie or something?"

They invite Charlie over after they get off work from the Sizzli Stick factory where they work for five bucks an hour when they rate themselves a 7 at best. They give him $20 to come back by with a movie and a stinky bag of popcorn because he burns through money quick.

Your first santa.

Hollywood & Charlie are in the mall around Christmas time.

Charlie: "What are we doing at the mall?"

Hollywood: "Go sit on Santa's lap."

Charlie walks over and sits on the santa's lap and quickly jumps back up and says "What the fuck that sick freak has a hard on?"

Hollywood: "That would be your first gay experience."

Chasity laughs "Gross."

Hollywood rolls her eyes at Chasity's comment. "Oh, come on, Chasity. Don't be such a prude. There's nothing wrong with being gay," she says with a smirk.

Charlie shoots Hollywood an annoyed look. "That's not the point," he says. "Why the hell did Santa have a hard-on? That's messed up."

Hollywood shrugs. "Who knows? Maybe it was just his candy cane poking out of his pocket," she jokes.

Charlie shakes his head in disbelief. "I can't believe I sat on that sick bastard's lap."

Chasity giggles. "Well, at least you'll have a good story to tell at parties," she says.

Hollywood grins mischievously. "Or we could use it to blackmail Santa for some extra presents this year."

Charlie rolls his eyes but can't help but chuckle at Hollywood's suggestion. "I don't think that's how it works, but sure, why not?"

As they walk out of the mall, Charlie can't shake the feeling of disgust from sitting on Santa's lap. But he knows he wouldn't trade his friends for anything in the world.

Hollywood chuckles in response to Chasity's remark. "Well, what did you expect, Charlie? It's not like Santa can control his bodily functions," he says with a sly grin.

Charlie rolls his eyes and crosses his arms. "Whatever, man. Let's just go get some food or something."

As they make their way through the mall, Chasity spots a cute guy working at one of the stores. She nudges Hollywood and points him out.

"Oh damn, he's cute," she whispers. "I wanna talk to him."

Hollywood smirks. "Go for it, girl. I'll go grab us a table at the food court."

Chasity takes a deep breath and walks over to the store. The cute guy greets her with a smile. "Hi there! Can I help you find anything?"

Chasity feels her heart racing as she looks into his eyes. "Uh, yeah...I was just wondering if you had any more of those scarves in the window display?"

He nods. "Sure thing, let me show you."

As they walk to the back of the store, Chasity can't help but feel a connection with him. They chat about their favorite movies and music as he helps her pick out a scarf.

After she pays and starts to leave the store, he grabs her hand and says, "Hey...would you maybe want to grab a coffee or something sometime?"

Chasity smiles and nods eagerly. "Yes! That sounds great."

Hollywood watches from afar with a grin on his face as Chasity walks back over to him.

As they walk away, Hollywood notices a man following them. He has a sinister expression on his face and seems to be getting closer with each step. Hollywood grabs Charlie's arm and pulls him into a department store.

"Hey man, what the hell?" Charlie protests.

"Shh," Hollywood whispers. "That guy was following us. We need to lose him."

They weave through the aisles, trying to blend in with the other shoppers. But the man is persistent and keeps closing in on them.

Hollywood spots an emergency exit door out of the corner of his eye. Without thinking twice, he grabs Charlie's hand and makes a run for it.

As they burst out into the back parking lot, Hollywood slams the door shut behind them and they catch their breath. The cold air stings their lungs as they try to slow down their racing heartbeats.

After a few minutes, they feel safe enough to make their way back toward the mall entrance. As they turn a corner, Hollywood notices that same man standing in front of them, blocking their path.

"Really?" Charlie mutters under his breath.

Hollywood steps in front of Charlie protectively. The stranger speaks up, "I'm not trying to hurt you guys. I saw the book you were carrying at the bookstore, and I just wanted to tell you it's my favorite too."

Hollywood relaxes slightly as he recognizes the book in question. He nods at the man and says "Oh man, yeah that's one of my favorites too."

Hollywood smirked at Chasity's reaction, knowing that she was just playing hard to get. He strolled over to Charlie, placing his hand on the small of his back, whispering in his ear, "Don't worry, I'll make it all better." With a quick wink at Chasity, Hollywood led Charlie towards a dimly lit corner of the mall.

Charlie's heart was pounding as Hollywood pushed him up against the wall. His breath caught in his throat as he felt Hollywood's lips press against his in a rough and passionate kiss. Hollywood's hands roamed over Charlie's body, tugging at his shirt and sliding down to his pants.

Just as things were getting heated, they were interrupted by a loud cough. They looked up to see Santa standing nearby with a stern expression on his face. "Gentlemen, this is not the place for that kind of behavior," he scolded before walking away.

Hollywood and Charlie both burst out laughing, not caring who heard them. It was just another wild night with their eccentric group of friends. As they continued their walk around the mall, holding hands and stealing kisses, Hollywood couldn't help but feel grateful for all the crazy adventures he shared with Charlie and their group of misfits. Life was never boring with them around.

Your first teacher.

Hollywood & Charlie are standing Charlie senior high school class.

Charlie: "What now?"

Hollywood: "Your teacher has a secret."

Charlie: "What secret?"

Hollywood: "You make her wet."

Charlie: "Yuck."

Hollywood: "You're gonna fail this class so maybe you should hook up with her so you'll pass."

Charlie: "I think I would rather fail."

Chasity laughs.

Hollywood: "And you wonder why you're still a virgin."

"I'm not a virgin. I've already had sex, you don't know what you talking about," Charlie said and laughed.

Hollywood: "Next time, try not to sound so confident about it. We were right, you failed. "

Charlie: "I know. Wanna go see a movie?"

Hollywood: "Let me go talk to my girl, hold on." Hollywood walked away and talked to his girl that was standing next to him the entire time. When he came back over towards Charlie he had a smile on his face and handed Charlie condoms in his jacket pockets. The two walked off towards Charlie car.

Charlie: "Why would you put condoms in my jackets?"

Hollywood: "Because we can't read the future and she might come back with us. Hollywood started laughing while he jumped into the passenger seat of Charlie's car while Charlie jumped into the driver seat. Hollywood started messing with Charlie which made him laugh as well.

Charlie: "Stop laughing, so what do you want to see?"

Hollywood: "You know exactly what I want to see, some white girl bootie."

Charlie: "HOLLYWOOD! STOP TALKING LIKE THAT WHEN WE PARKED AT THE MOVIES! We got out the car and headed inside; I bought us tickets as we headed around trying to find a good seat. I popped some popcorn and brought it over towards where Hollywood sat when we heard balloons being blown up.

Charlie: "Well, I'm gonna do better today. I really am."

Hollywood: "And this time I want to see a little ass."

Charlie: "You're gonna make her wet."

Hollywood: "You going to do it?"

Charlie: "Well, maybe she has something for me actually, some notes or something."

Chasity laughs.

Charlie stands in front of the class. Charlie looks at his wet teacher Avery. She takes off her sweater to reveal she is wearing a flesh-colored negligee underneath where her nipples are seen poking through to her students' delight as they groan in jealousy and longing for that same experience. She sits on the desk next to Charlie so they are both facing the class and puts an arm around his shoulders like they are lovers walking on the beach under the stars and he whispers in her ear from behind where no one can hear what he says to only her ears and then she slaps him hard across the face unexpectedly drawing a straight line of blood along his cheek like a streak of lipstick bleeding under his eye which causes everyone in the class to gasp sounding like one huge gulping orgasmic breath exhaled as a single unified moan for sure because now he is forever captured by the imagination of his peers and for certain because they will always be heard and forever known as Chuckles until he finally dies just as if Charlie was shot while standing on stage at Madison Square Garden and fell over dead onto the microphone where he was making such an amazing apology anticipating a standing ovation call.

Charlie: "I don't want it anyway."

Hollywood: "You didn't want that cat either but you got him."

Chasity laughs.

Hollywood: "What's her name?"

Charlie: "Victoria."

Hollywood: "Lets go ask where she is."

Charlie follows Hollywood into the school hallway.

Hollywood: "Yo Victoria, Victoria!"

Several students stop what they are doing to stare at them. The stare loudly and wild at them.

Hollywood: "Hey Victoria, hey Victoria! Where is she?"

Victoria is in a classroom and stares outside the door seeing Hollywood and Charlie talking and waving her hand at the classroom window. Hollywood turns his head to see her behind him. He waves back at her and runs to the class door. He knocks on it and opens the door walking into the class. Chasity stays outside the class looking for Victoria or better yet, any other suitable girl in the classroom uncomfortable that he doesn't have a plan or know what to do without going up to a potential lady in his head spinning completely unprepared like Charlie does not prepared even after he takes over his body. Hollywood walks towards Victoria who is sitting next to black guy on a desk who nonchalantly gives his seat to him. He sits down and talks in his own language, she laughs..

Victoria: "So you on your way now? It was only one time... I can safely say that whatever just happened was not natural given everyone.

Charlie: "Hey. I'm average at best."

Hollywood: "That's not what I hear."

Charlie: "What do you hear?" Hollywood: "Magic Johnson could not get his pole into you."

Charlie: "But Little John Reed that guy half my size found his way in, easy peasy!"

Chasity laughs over Charlie's class joke. Hollywood: "Why is it that the lower your IQ is the more sex you have?"

Charlie: "I don't know... That would be Stupid."

Charlie & Chasity laughing Hollywood: (chuckles)

Hollywood: "Well, if I hear anything else I'll let ya know." Charlie: "Thanks man."

Your first roommate.

Hollywood & Charlie are in Charlie's apartment.

Charlie: "What's Darren, doing here?"

Hollywood: "He's your first roommate."

Darren: "I care about you Charlie, I want you."

Charlie: "What?"

Darren: "You don't pay enough attention to me Charlie, Let's make out."

Charlie: "Huh?"

Hollywood: "Did I mention Darren is a raging homo?"

Darren: "I am not gay." Starts crying.

Chasity: "I think it's someone's time of the month, does he need a tampon?"

Darren: "Carly, I'm not gay and I'm not on my time of the month."

Hollywood: "This gives me an idea folks. Charlie hikes up Darren's shirt to revealing a massive set of breast, no nipples just breast."

Charlie: "Wow these are big. I mean look at these on you, I mean look at them. You are such a pretty boy, I mean guy."

Darren: "I'm glad you like them Charlie, I paid a lot for them too, remember? Let me put tongues with you."

Charlie: "Huh?"

Hollywood: "Obviously Charlie thinks that Darren had his breasts surgically removed and the fake ones put it. Dar reminds Charlie about the boob job he gave him in their freshman year at college. Even though they have been roommates for three years and their friendship grew the size of these beasts while at a Halloween party in 99', apparently, Charlie forgot about it till now!"

Darren: "Why are you scared of me, of us? We're best friends! Friends hug each other and become awkward with each other all the time! Let me franchise my bud!"

Charlie: "Go franchise yourself. Both of you lesbians need to bounce now before I scream rape! And it would be a false charge because I told you both that this was my apartment!"

Hollywood: "It's not that bad." Hollywood gets on his phone and calls the landlord.

Darren: "I am not a homo, I just want you to pay attention to me."

The Landlord: "I am sorry Charlie your sharing with Darren, you can have one more roommate, but that's it."

Charlie: Whatever. (throwing Our Riot Cell phone in her purse)

House of Angola: Angola opens the door to her dorm room. Her best friend Malita is standing in the doorway.

Angola: "For real? All my life you said you were my friend and this what you do to me." (grabbing her wrecked painting on on the wall) .

Tia: "We are done!"

Angola: "I don't know why I wasted my time with you all this time! You are full of shit! Now i am going to walk that Walk Of Shame and shoot myself instead of having slutty ways with Fallacy first year."

Tia: "Oh shut up...is he here? I bet him I end it first ." Malita peeks into the room. Really its empty .

Angola puts her boots on "Let me atleast give him his presents before some old ugly whore snag him up now that he is legally defenseless! What a waste of a great boi like that! Damn Fallacy is really dumb!" Angola storms out of their Dorm room.

Darren: "NO! (ttyl)"

Charlie (kicking Darren out): "I just do not have the time for all this drama! I have to follow my dreams."

Hollywood: "It's about time Charlie, good luck with putting your life back together."

Charlie: "Thank you Hollywood, for everything. You are the best!"

Chasity: "Take a picture of us in the new apartment, don't I look cute?"

Charlie: "Yes you are sweetie, let me take your photo. What are your dreams Chasity? You could be anything, anything at all!"

Chasity: "I want to be a pioneer!" Blows a bubble.

Carpenter: "How now, brown cow?" Starts sawing something as Charlie and Hollywood run away...in the wrong direction...away from the carpenter...home to find more meat for their babies...

Darren: "Holly, that was rude."

Hollywood: "Thanks, but no."

Darren: "Aww why does Holly not want my vagina?"

Charlie: "Shut up Darren!"

Chasity: "Charlie this is your house too, I'll let you fight over this."

Charlie: "That's fine with me. I would rather have Craig as a roommate than some crazy homo! and that's homophobic hate speech."

Darren: "Wait one second, what? I love women... and men! Androgynous men who wear make-up! I am a lesbigay transwoman! So it is you who are gay. But I also love straight women and literally every gender despite their preferences!" Looks at Charlie. "You deny your own nature just so people can perceive you as straight. It's fucking stupid, babe." Starts crying again.

Craig wanders out of his room to see the commotion.

CRAIG: "What the fuck is going on? Darren stop crying or I will kick your ass right now... mostly for being embarrassing but also for thinking shithead products are an investment strategy. Look, Darren, if you need attention there are plenty of other ways to get it like getting a cat... or having sex with someone who actually wants to have sex with you instead of manipulating them for money and pretending that all sex is somehow emotionally fulfilling because that's how God wired you.

Your first bully.

Hollywood & Charlie are in a store.

Jennifer walks up to Charlie and kisses him and says "Wow you got cute."

Charlie: "Do I know you?"

Jennifer: "Yes but I looked different back then."

Charlie: "What do you mean?"

Hollywood: "You dumbass she means she was James before she had the sex change to become Jennifer."

Charlie pukes.

Chasity: "Eww."

Hollywood: "At least you know why she was a bully back then because she wanted your dick."

Charlie: "My dick?"

Jennifer: "Yesssssssss!"

Charlie screams and runs out of the store.

Jennifer: "Cum get it!!!"

Hollywood is on the phone with David. He is in a field talking to him. Hollywood talks to David and then leans back and sees a car coming towards them, in the back seat was a tied up Cassie. Hollywood notices the car up the road. He casually leans back again and is hit by a truck that smashes into the driver side door of his truck. The impact sends him rolling down a big hill on top of one of his tires at the bottom of the hill with massive damage to his truck. The truck crashes into a building causing a giant hole into it as it stops from sliding further in to it. The building has flooded water from the busted pipe inside the garage attached to the building. Hollywood is knocked out from hitting his head so hard on the steering wheel. The last person he would have expected shows up at the scene from what he last knew about her before she went missing comes out of her car and walks over to him with a gun in her hand and now hates Hollywood after what he had done to Cassie. David walks around Hollywood's truck looking for him when, Suddenly, he sees her standing by his truck. He freezes in fear not believing who he was standing face to face with but before he does anything stupid she pulls out her gun and shoots him 4 times in the chest, once in each shoulder & hip. As David falls he takes one long look at her before she shoots.

Josiah walks by and says "I don't remember."

Hollywood: "Yeah you remember. You called her Jamesy before she became Jennifer."

James: "Yea I'm disgusted and repulsed with myself."

Jennifer: "Don't worry you're not the first person to not know or remember my true past. James was my aunt, my sister, a girl we used to bully and shit but now I'm back in his body baby so be nice to me. Yea I got the balls to wear that pink dress with sneakers but at least I'm honest about being gay unlike the fakes in Hollywood. They are good people but I wish they'd stop trying to pretend love is in fashion but it's not man. Gay is the new straight so if your gonna be gay be gay damnit and if you dont like it then go fuck yourself move out of my way please."

Chasity: "Thank you for giving Harvey a home. I want you all to meet our puppy named Harvey..."

Chasity pulls down her pants and shit falls out all over Hollywood's shoes as well as Jennifer's dress shoes.

Chasity drops the dog on top of everything and I pee on Josiah's shoe as a sign of anger! (Wolf Smell)

Hollywood: "Oh no I think there dead. Oh wait... no they isn't, they just sleeping off rainbows when you have sex without a condom like Romeo & Juliet all over my mommy's favorite carpet flooding this house!

Jennifer: "Actually it was Britney."

Charlie: "Awe."

Hollywood: "You're fucking gay Charlie."

Chasity grabs Charlie and Hollywood by their hands and starts leading them out.

The song is in a nother language and is sung by Jennifer. She says: The girl her is going to go on a date now. And he will lose his mind when he sees how beautiful she is. He will think I am too good for him but I don't care everyone knows that I am just as good as the rest of you. Oh yes I am just as good as the rest of you

The song ends while we see Charlie and Hollywood trying their best to pee standing up when they get back to the motel room or just mess it all up in their pants. Chasity is all clean because she has potty trained herself from believing she has to wear diapers again and drinks out of regular bowls and cups just like a big girl now instead of always going on pee or poop accidents because she believes that she has to wear diapers thanks to her brother Melvin forcing her to wear diapers even after she became potty trained in order to make her act "Chasity like a baby girl dear sweet sweet Chasity" so when they finally pee themselves while standing up at the bar here in <somewhere?> they have braces on their legs so they are chained together with Chasity being able to go pee then so we can all see each other peeing for the first time before hiding behind an asteroid until the spaceship lands in a corn field.

J: "I was a bitch?"

H: "Yeah you were with those sunglasses all the time and wore all black. It's because you wanted to look like a goth chick."

Chasity: "You told me boys liked girls like that."

J: "You tried to get with Hollywood back then too. You wanted to take him home and mommy fucked you up your ass and now Hollywood is with me."

J: "I will need to fuck your boyfriend before I let you go out on a date with him."

Chasity: "No I don't want an abortion, but thanks for the offer."

J: "If I have to pay to help you raise him then I will make sure you never see the light of day again."

Mackenzie: "Come on honeypack lets go home."

Hollywood stares down Jennifer and says "we would date if you weren't a whore so why don't you go fuck up someone else's life since my wife doesn't need your sloppy seconds or hours."

Chasity pulls Hollywood out of the store by his shirt collar. She grabs the baby from Mackenzie's hands and goes outside of the store before slamming it shut behind Hollywood and not giving a rip about security in the store calling any kids paying for their dolls or toys inside. Chasity just ignored everyone screaming at her for not following mall's rules about security checks and very few people can call that lady out though to say she is.

Your first crazy friend.

Hollywood & Charlie are in the backyard.

Brad: "Hey Charlie?"

Charlie: "What Brad?"

Brad: "Watch what I can do."

Charlie: "Ok."

Brad jumps on the trampoline and tries to do a backflip and racks himself on the metal bar and screams.

Chasity laughs.

Charlie: "Ouch."

Hollywood: "Congratulations you're an idiot."

Brad: "Yeah yeah."

___

(The night of the party.)

Forever: "Hollywood you look great tonight."

Hollywood: "Thanks."

Forever: "I got you a gift."

Hollywood: "Ok lets see what you got me."

Forever: "It's a necklace."

Hollywood takes it and tries it on and it is so pink you can clearly see it from the moon.

Hollywood: "Wow thanks!"

Forever: "Do they have this color in my size? This wouldn't be caught dead on me?"

Hollywood: "Well it looks good on you and the color is so pretty!"

Forever: "Yeah but I would never wear this color, but thanks anyway Hollywood I love you!"

Chasity: "Charlie's really smart sometimes."

Brad: "Hey check it out how do I get- going-man-down-that kills.-uh embrace-tastiness."

Charlie: "I'm cool like that."

Hollywood: "Do you even know what I just said?"

Charlie looks at Hollywood then back at Brad and Chasity.

Chasity: "His flip was garbage. Brad win! "

Brad: "Yeah win win."

****

In the living room, Erin, Jason, Brittany and Caleb are in the living room eating popsicles. They were playing games on the iPad and just hung out talking.

On the iPad 2 Brittany is playing a female version of Bejeweled. Her piece spins around and when it lands it must match 3 other pieces of the same color to get points. Erin is watching her play as does Caleb. Jason has his headphones on listening to his music on his iPhone 4S which is laying on a pillow in his lap propped up by his hands. He had been lost in thought staring at Nathan Gale coming through the attic window on his horror movie startling him jolting him back into reality. The air blue frosted iPod docking station turned on and Jason turned up J Cole's song A Tale of 2 Citiez loud making Brittany startled and jump turning her grumpy face back to smiling bright as she hummed along to this song enjoying herself again like always while she played with Nathan Gale one handed holding...

Brad: "Funny."

Brad screams again.

Hollywood: "You're an idiot!"

All of us are laughing.

Charlie: "You're either pretty dumb or pretty brave doing that."

Brad: "Or both."

Charlie: "Yeah you're right it was probably a combo of both."

All of us laugh again.

Paris & Chasity come back with a TV dinner scared and eyes wide open, startled.

Paris & Chasity scream.

Chasity: "What are you guys doing?!"

Hollywood, Charlie & Brad: "JUMPING ON THE TRAMPOLINE!"

Chasity: "Guys you just ruptured Brad in the butt hole area!"

Hollywood, Charlie & Brad: *Laughing Multiple Stops*

Paris: "Oh my gosh I saw a flying cauldron or something! A cauldron! A cauldron with wings! And I thought what is going on? He must be high like an insect, and he is high and having an episode! It looked like a flying rug with wings! And I don't know what he is talking about because it didn't have rug this lady pulled on a flying broomstick tap dancing on sunshine flapping her wings until she felt physics took over and fell backwards landing in her little puddle cup of green tea and left eleven feathers behind...and that was so weird and why is she dancing on... nevermind.

Brad: "Thanks."

Chasity: "What was that?"

Brad: "I'm sore."

Charlie: *rolls eyes* 'Whatever.'

Chasity: *Sarcastically* "Oh poor Brad."

Brad: *Rolls eyes* "You think you know so much. Let me ask you this. Whatever happened to the green Ranger?"

Hollywood & Charlie stare blankly at him and Hollywood finally answers.

"He quit." Hollywood said.

Brad: "Well why didn't you save the park?."

Hollywood and Charlie stared blankly at him as they were confused why he was asking them that question about why didn't they save the carnival park.

Chasity saw emotion on Brad's face from asking the question about what happened with the park in which she can see that he really really cares about it so she decide to answer for them and let him know what happened to it in which she gives a stiff look towards Hollywood & Charlie as they realize why she looked at them that way.

"Listen Brad, Donny used to tell me how he use to have a great time growing up here on the carnival park and now because of....them it's all over." Chasity said pointing to her brother & sister-in-law. "The park closed down, people lost their jobs, everything was destroyed, and there is no longer a carnival park." She added.

Your first addiction.

Hollywood & Charlie are in Jory's apartment.

Jory is sitting on the sofa playing games on the wii and eating pizza.

Charlie: "Why are we at Jory's apartment?"

Hollywood: "Your first addiction was video games."

Jory: "Hey Charlie you want to play with my wii?"

Charlie: "No thanks."

Hollywood: "Jory has a few addictions. Video games, food and dick."

Chasity: "The only way the wii can get gayer is if they name the next one the weenie."

Charlie rolled his eyes at Hollywood's comment. He didn't need to know about Jory's personal life, let alone his preferences. He headed over to the kitchen, hoping to find something to drink. As he opened the fridge, he caught a glimpse of something that made him do a double take.

"Uh, Hollywood?" Charlie called out, trying to keep his voice steady.

"What is it?" Hollywood asked, walking over to the kitchen. His eyes followed Charlie's gaze to where he was pointing.

Jory had left a pack of condoms right in the middle of the fridge.

Charlie looked over at Jory, who was still engrossed in his game. "What's up with that?"

Hollywood shrugged. "Maybe he's planning on getting lucky tonight."

Charlie raised an eyebrow. "With who?"

As if on cue, Chasity walked into the apartment. She sauntered over to Jory and sat down next to him on the couch. "Hey guys," she greeted them.

Charlie couldn't help but notice the way Jory's eyes lit up at her presence. He then turned his attention back to the fridge and grabbed a beer. Maybe he should just mind his own business and enjoy his night off.

Jory looked up from his game and laughed at Chasity's joke. Hollywood rolled her eyes while Charlie nervously chuckled. The tension in the room was palpable, but Jory seemed unfazed.

Jory: "Hey, no need to be shy Charlie. You can join in on the fun."

Charlie's face turned red as he shook his head.

Charlie: "I think I'll pass."

Hollywood smirked as she leaned in closer to Charlie.

Hollywood: "Are you afraid you won't be able to handle it? Jory here is quite skilled with his joystick."

Charlie's heart rate quickened as he felt a rush of arousal wash over him. He had never been with a man before, but the thought of Jory's expertise sent shivers down his spine.

Jory patted the seat next to him on the sofa.

Jory: "Come on, Charlie. I promise you won't regret it."

Charlie hesitated for a moment before finally giving in to his desires. He sat down next to Jory and picked up a controller.

As they played their game, Jory's hand rested on Charlie's thigh, inching closer and closer to his crotch. Charlie tried to focus on the game, but his body was on fire with anticipation.

Finally, Jory leaned in and whispered in Charlie's ear.

Jory: "Let's take this to the bedroom."

Charlie nodded eagerly as they both got up from the sofa and left Hollywood and Chasity behind, lost in another world of their own.

Hollywood rolled her eyes at Chasity's crass comment. She didn't know why she bothered hanging out with these people. But then again, it was all part of the job.

She turned her attention back to Jory, who was still munching on pizza and tapping buttons on his Wii remote. She couldn't help but notice how seductive he looked, with his tousled hair and lazy grin. She wondered if he would be up for a little fun.

Hollywood cleared her throat. "Hey Jory, you wanna play a different kind of game?"

Jory looked up at her, intrigued. "What kind of game?"

Hollywood smirked. "A game where we don't use controllers."

Jory's eyes widened as he caught on to what she was implying. He set down the Wii remote and stood up, revealing a sizable bulge in his sweatpants.

Chasity groaned and rolled her eyes. "Ugh, can't you guys do that somewhere else? I'm trying to eat my pizza in peace."

Charlie chuckled nervously. "Yeah, let's give them some privacy."

Hollywood grabbed Jory by the hand and led him to his bedroom, closing the door behind them. She wasted no time in tearing off his clothes and climbing on top of him.

It wasn't long before they were both panting and moaning with pleasure.

Meanwhile, Chasity and Charlie finished their pizza in silence, both feeling a bit left out.

As soon as Chasity made her comment, Hollywood and Charlie burst out laughing. Jory rolled his eyes and continued to munch on his pizza.

Hollywood: "Speaking of dick, Jory, we need to talk about something."

Jory raised an eyebrow curiously. He put down his pizza slice and turned off his Wii.

Jory: "What is it?"

Hollywood: "We have a new job for you."

Charlie: "We need you to seduce a wealthy businessman's son. We need to get our hands on some important documents he has in his possession."

Jory sighed. He knew what that meant.

Jory: "How much are you offering?"

Hollywood smirked.

Hollywood: "Enough for you to buy all the pizza and video games in the world."

Jory grinned back at him.

Jory: "Deal."

Chasity watched as the three men began discussing their plan in detail. She knew better than to interfere with their work, but she couldn't help but feel a little left out.

Chasity: "So, what am I supposed to do in all of this?"

Hollywood turned to her with a serious look on his face.

Hollywood: "Your job is to distract the businessman while Jory does his thing with the son."

Chasity nodded, understanding her role in the mission.

Chasity: "Got it. So when do we start?"

Charlie glanced at his watch.

Charlie: "In 2 days. We need to prepare for this."

Your first stalker.

Hollywood & Charlie are in Charlie's high school for the prom.

Fat Girl walks up to Charlie and says "Hi Charlie."

Charlie looks at Fat Girl and jumps back and says "Holy crap you're ugly."

Fat Girl: "I'll let you fuck me in all 3 holes if you'll be my prom date."

Charlie: "Who are you?"

Hollywood: "She's Shamu's fatter uglier sister, no she's Dan's sister."

Charlie: "That explains the ugliness, Look blubber butt I refuse to lower my standards so up yours."

Chasity laughs.

Fat Girl: "You suck." Walks away.

Fat girl takes the stage. "Ladies and Gentlemen, we have the winner of the Prom Queen pageant, Tammy Pouch."

Shamu and his buddies come from nowhere. "Well, that was easy."

Tammy starts crying as she's being crowned.

Fat Girl comforts Tammy: "Don't cry, you could always be my cuddle buddy when I'm lonely." Tiffany starts crying. "No one will ever love me cuz I have this fat ass."

Padre Puno is double fisting Rabbi 9-inch Star Wars action figures to Jackoff Jackson. Izzy Wiener is doing tequila shots and when that jar is empty he goes back for more tequila. Bruno Mooner takes a crap in his pants and didn't even know it until it was all said and done.

Charlie walks up to Chasity and asks her, hey baby, "What's shakin'?"

Chasity: "It isn't so much shakin' as it is fuckin'."

Hollywood & Charlie turn around and see The Dales.

Hollywood: "Charlie we can coerce them into being in our movie. If we have a movie title I can write the script."

Chasity: "How about Parental Advisory that fits all the time, and goes step beyond you and 1 or more of you could or can get it slapped onto you by a judge if you have sex with a mentally-handicapped individual."

Charlie: "Yeah that sounds good what?"

Hollywood: "I was thinking PG-13 because it has sex, violence and language in it knowing Hollywood he would probably put sex, violence, bad language, 3-way nudity, and a blow job into it.

They walk into the cafeteria: Charlie sees Kids playing basketball on the court and asks who they are. Some kid says they are there for the All Star game all stars vs the JV all stars. He asks who won the last game and they say the JVs were so bad that most of them quit playing basketball after they lost to all stars since most of them have career aspirations where not being good at basketball would hurt their chances of being successful in other areas. Charlie looks around at kids eating lunch with everyone staring at him so he sits at his table on the same side as Hollywood.

Chasity: "For the record if anyone cares I think you dropped to a C."

Hollywood & Charlie: "Ew"

Hollywood: "How big are you?"

Charlie: "My dick is so small that the sprinkler system thinks I'm retired and doesn't water my lawn."

Hollywood: "She likes the way you suck cock, she'll be eating fried chicken for a month now."

Charlie starts laughing.

Hollywood: "Alexis party tonight? Want me to bring the Kodiak? I got some [Medina hops] at that other liquor store yesterday. We could get drunk as shit on Hop nip and you can have sex with every girl in this room. Get them all pregnant too while we're at it. You down?"

Charlie looks around the room, looking for chicks.

Charlie: "Sure, I guess. Let's have sex as soon as possible, I mean as long as everyone else agrees with it yeah fuck yeah that sounds like a great great idea for that! My God, we should get a like a live studio audience over here and do a fucking party!

Hollywood: "Only if you pay for it or your dad does, because there is no fucking way I am paying for it Brosephus."

Charlie: "I'm gay babe."

Fat Girl is standing at the punch bowl talking with boys:

Fat Girl: "So do you boys like eating pussy?"

Boys: "We love it."

Fat Girl: "Have you guys ever eaten a pussy where the clit was huge and almost touchable?"

Boys: "No but we would love to."

Fat Girl: "Can you feel my phaser in your neck?"

The boys nod scared.

Fat Girl: "Good cause I have someone to meet, if I were you I would go stand somewhere else." Walks off.

Girls walking down the hall while a guy runs up behind them and grabs their asses. Fat Girl looks down and around at everyone who runs away fast. Fat girl walks over to the guy that did it. Fat girl gets her fat walk going and starts swinging her hip from side to side as she approaches the guy trying to run away. The girls look on in awe.

Fat girl gets real close to the guy and says loud enough for everyone around to hear: "What's shakin buns? Why did we stop shaking them in the bathroom? you know what I'm talking about when we were peeing and rubbing our crack together while peeing in the lake causing it not to splash up on us.

Chasity: "Told you so."

Charlie: "Oh shut up."

Fat Girl sits down and Hollywood sits down beside her.

Fat Girl: "What are you doing? I don't wanna talk to you."

Hollywood: "Why not?"

Fat Girl: "I know you just wanna fuck me and get out. Your all the same."

Hollywood: *pulls Fat Girl into his lap* "I'll prove it to you then. Look, get here early tomorrow during lunch and if I ever followed through on something, it's that I will meet you out in the parking lot to show you something that will get you into Cal Poly Pomona."

Fat girl: "Umm..okay sure thing... Stop rubbing on me. I can feel your hard-on through your pants! Ew! Disgusting! Gross!"

Hollywood looks down at his jeans and sees some shit on his pants and jumps back.

Hollywood: 'Fuck I need a new pair of jeans..maybe three days from now there will be a sale at the mall and spencers or something sure hope so at least till then my dick is gonna be in pain then...'

Fuck how did that happen....the toilets are probably clogged...fucking pay toilet never have any change. No wonder why everyone says south bay sucks...that does suck btw...so many stupid fucking star bucks everywhere...this place kinda just reminds me of Vegas...

Charlie: "Hey Lights!"

Lights: "Yeah?"

Charlie: "I gotta tell you man, that was a good idea. I mean there was no way I was ever going to the prom with her."

Lights: "Well you would've been a fool to go out with her, it could have ruined your perfect record."

Hollywood walks up to Charlie and says "Hey Dick has been sitting in this corner right here for the last like 4 hours waiting for his date, in that tie he's wearing he already looks retarded."

Charlie: "Oh my God, everyone is going to make fun of him because of that tie and I'm not going to be able to watch it."

Lights: "He also smells like Old Spice—which stinks more than the stank ass feet of a couple hobos covered in shit and dead animals."

Charlie: "You're fucking brutal Lights. But that piece of information might have just saved his life, lucky for him there isn't a girl who would still go out with him after that tie. Maybe less fortunate for Mr Shit feet here but Dick being Dick is still going to wonder all night why she stood him up. My head hurts like a motherfucker from all the laughing on the yacht but man this is better than TV or video games. This is real Frank, this moment we are living in right now will remain forever etched in my mind and no one can take this away from us.

Your first stupid friend.

Hollywood & Charlie are in Dan's apartment.

Dan is sitting in a game chair playing Xbox 360.

Charlie: "Why are we at Dan's apartment?"

Hollywood: "So, you can learn from his mistakes."

Dan: "Hey Charlie, guess what I did last night?"

Hollywood: "Fucked a blow up doll causing it to come to life so it could kill itself."

Chasity laughs.

Charlie: "What Dan?"

Dan: "I went a WWE event and I had sex with the divas and I kicked all the guys in the nuts and ran away."

Hollywood: "How did he manage to have sex when his dick ran away from home the first time it saw him? Oh he's the new Lorena Bobbitt, he stole someone's dick."

Charlie: "Dan, that's gross."

Hollywood: "No, that's Dan."

Dan: "No, that's basketball. I got I got choked and hit my face but it was cool you should try it it's a new feeling call uh bloodperts (?) because when he gets hit in the nuts he drops a...this is what would happen if you could do basketball.. okay if there was this laser space gun..."

Hollywood: "He ain't making any sense man"

Dan: "Come on Hollywood don't listen to Cameron how many times have you been hit in the nuts."

Hollywood: "I walked in front of a weight room door once and thought I hadn't seen it coming when really it had come at me super fast. It still hurts to walk sometimes and probably also runs damage to my future children as well."

Dan: [laughter] "That is the most bizarre metaphor I have ever heard. Sheets what did you do last night? You were supposed to have sex weren't you? Did you fucking cum? You said this is your fifteen minutes of fame ran out so fast. What happened? You didn't even get laid? What fucking happened? Did you run away like they did with felonies mommy not gonna let me do anything fun anymore.

Charlie: "Kane's mask is on too tight. He should have let Ultimate Warrior give him some steroids."

Hollywood: "Warrior was fired as the security guy at Dairy Queen because he stole all the Blizzards. It's like 20 years now and he's still trying to sell them on eBay."

Charlie: "Warrior should have been the next Randy Savage."

Dan: "Randy Savage is dead people."

Chasity: "Savage would suck a gorilla cock for a million dollars. We have all seen his bare ass so we know his hole is big enough to do it."

Hollywood: "I bet if you scrolled through Savage's phone it would say, 'DUNN DUNN DUNN DUNNNN!!!!!...... DUNN! DUNN! DUNN! DUNN!... Hey Snake! This is Randy, I'm rentin-a-car!' Text Randy Savage for last minute reservations for weddings! Or send a Christmas card to Randy Cuntcunt!! Or if you need any custom erotic stories or erotic fiction. Send $3 to Randy Savage and include your name and where you want him to tell you he fucked invisible traffic cones on your chest with invisible soprano penis."

Dan: "If that really does say that on his phone then why doesn't he just use a regular phone?"

Hollywood & Charlie laugh. Chasity begins to weep.

Dan: "It was amazing, it's like a bad acid trip man."

Hollywood: "You're still off it, aren't you?"

Dan: "No, but I would be if Shaun Hardy hadn't taken me cold and sober."

Charlie: "Who is Shaun Hardy?"

Dan: "Dude! He trains Brock Lesnar! He told me he saw me on my first hooker and asked if he could be my best friend and then he gave me a place to sleep for the night! Tosh.0 was there! And she hooked me up too. That woman is a saint! And let me tell you she has one of the most kick ass bodies you could ever imagine! She makes Madison look like an ant by comparison. It's insane! All of them make Melanie greener than grass looking like an ant. You don't know what your missing guys...it really is worth going sober if it will get you that as a side effect."

His personality switches from that of a human being to that of a Zoidberg Fish Person from Futurama. (Holding his hands out like claws) "So, I want you to give me all your money or I will kill you with this gun, but the money is more important, cause money can buy pills with which can make me feel better about some things in life like death and disappointment but also disappointment.

Hollywood and Dan laugh.

Charlie: "So, um, why are we here?"

Hollywood: "Because you're grown up now and you deserve money to go to a WWE event so I'm here to watch you spend your money. Your allowance is your spending money so you can go eat out at restaurants from college now. You don't have to ask mom or dad for money."

Charlie: "Awesome! Thank you!"

Chasity: "Thanks Hollywood."

Hollywood: "Feel like going to a barber type outfit place first? We could make you all hipster and shit and I could get a haircut too. It would be fun because we can talk about countdowns, top tens, throwing the first stone, and create our own wrestling dynasty."

Charlie: "We can use this money to go to another event too! Who knows what we will see if we go again?"

Chasity: "Sounds like more of a plan Hollywood. I got the rest of the day off from work today so I can go hang out with my sister instead of being an anti-social bitch all day. So what do you say Dan? Want to come out with everyone today? You can buy lunch if it makes you feel better and makes us show up quicker."

Your first day of college.

Hollywood & Charlie are at Charlie's college.

Charlie: "Why are we at college?"

Hollywood: "It's your first day of college."

Charlie: "Cool."

Hollywood: "You get kicked out of college tomorrow."

Charlie: "Why?"

Hollywood: "The dean's daughter wanted you to fuck her but you said no."

Charlie: "I'll have to remember to say yes next time."

Hollywood: "You'll also have to remember to put a bag over her head."

Edward: "Charlie, get your feet off the table."

Hollywood: "Get your dad's gun and shoot Charlie's adopted brother."

Edward: "You've been adopted?"

Charlie: "He chew my homework."

Edward: "And I've been an asshole."

Hollywood: "It's time for you to do your chores. You have to mopy about having to mopy about your chores while you mop the floors and I mop over with the rocks in Hollywood still trying to find something to cheer you up. And then Chinatown and you know what they say about big mops right? Big ... well use your imagination, it's crude but works. And then Dad has to work late so you and Edward are going to get drunk because Edward has teacher burnout syndrome again even though he always enjoys hitting on his hot female students. And we'll end on a screwed-up note because all the best comedies end on a screwed up note ending, ae-ae-a-ae-aae – (Hands lowered) ... Boom! Special effect! There you go. Charlie, are you done eating your toothpaste? When we go home (?)

"I guess this is our foyer." said the Dean, sticking his dick in a hole that they had dug out of the ground.

"This must be our house. We forgot to pay the mortgage again, right?" said Charlie as he knelt down to tie his shoe laces.

Dee leaned forward and shouted, "Vern!" to get his attention before she kicked him in the nuts with her heels. The Vern's face turned red and he squinted, then threw up on himself, collapsing to his knees and coughing up chunks of half-digested scrambled eggs. Dee darted out the room and went for the front door. Charlie tried to keep up but nearly tripped over Vern who was throwing up in the corner near the bed. Loser Puck grabbed Charlie's pant leg and pulled him down into a bear hug as he vomited copiously into Charlie's shorts (which were made entirely out of vomit from Puck). Mr. Connor giggled hysterically at Charlie as Vern finished puking up what appeared to be a yellow slurry of shit and horrible morning breath all over the carpet. On the floor between them was a box with four large cocks sticking out of it.

Hollywood helps him cover up rape. Continue.

Charlie: "So what did I do instead?"

Hollywood: "Went and got your haircut."

Charlie: "What kind of haircut?"

Hollywood: "Letterman haircut."

Charlie: "I ain't wearing a bag over my head for anyone or any haircut."

Eyes cast upwards while smiling. Slight shrug. Slight tilt of the head to the right. The only curse a man who ruled the world under movie director Leni Riefenstahl could know was a shoulder shrug followed by small smile. Learn how to be cool from Hollywood, my Charlie Bronson readers.

Hollywood: "Neil was there too!"

Charlie: "Why was Neil there?"

I thought I told you not to read that! ... Look in yourself, Eddie baby! ... We Must Kill all the White People and Drink Their Blood... I thought I told you not to read ... that!

Your first job.

Hollywood & Charlie are in an office.

Charlie: "Why are we in an office?"

Hollywood: "It's your first job."

Charlie: "Oh."

Hollywood: "You're the new president of circuit city."

Charlie: "Cool."

Hollywood: "The bad news is they went broke so you have to find a new job."

Charlie: "That sucks."

Hollywood watched as Charlie slumped down into his chair, a look of disappointment etched across his face. She knew that she had to do something to help him out. "Don't worry," she said reassuringly. "I have a job offer for you."

Charlie perked up, intrigued by what Hollywood had to say. "What is it?" he asked eagerly.

"It's a position at a startup," she replied. "They're looking for someone with your skills and experience."

"That sounds great," Charlie exclaimed. "Tell me more."

Hollywood smiled, happy to see the excitement in Charlie's eyes. "It's a company that specializes in virtual reality technology," she explained. "They're doing some really groundbreaking work in the field."

Charlie's eyes widened with interest. Virtual reality was something that he had always been fascinated by, and the chance to work in that field was too good to pass up.

"I'm definitely interested," he said decisively.

"Excellent," Hollywood replied, beaming with pride at her protégé. "I'll set up an interview for you tomorrow."

Charlie nodded eagerly, feeling a sense of hope and excitement wash over him. Thanks to Hollywood's guidance, he was on his way to finding his dream job.

Hollywood leaned back in his chair, feeling the weight of the news he had just delivered to his protege. Charlie seemed like a good kid, but Hollywood knew that this news would be a true test of his character.

"You know what, Charlie," Hollywood said with a grin as he stood up from his chair. "I've got an idea."

Charlie raised an eyebrow at his mentor's sudden enthusiasm. "What kind of idea?"

"We're going to start our own company," Hollywood declared, throwing his arms wide in excitement. "We'll be the biggest thing Silicon Valley has ever seen!"

Charlie looked skeptical, but couldn't help feeling a quickening of his heart at the prospect of starting his own business. "What kind of company?"

"An app," Hollywood said simply. "The next big thing."

Charlie nodded slowly, thinking it over. Starting their own company was a risky venture, but it was also exciting. He trusted Hollywood's judgment and knew that he would do anything to support him in this new endeavor.

"Let's do it," Charlie said finally, a determined look in his eyes.

And so the two set to work, pouring hours of time and energy into developing their new app. It wasn't easy - there were long nights and plenty of setbacks - but they were determined to make it work.

Finally, after months of hard work and dedication, their app was ready for launch.

"Hollywood, we did it," Charlie breathed as they watched the download count skyrocket on their phones.

"We did," Hollywood agreed with a proud smile. "And it's only the beginning."

Hollywood nodded sympathetically. "Yeah, it does. But don't worry, I've got something else lined up for you."

Charlie raised an eyebrow. "What kind of job?"

Hollywood leaned back in his chair, steepling his fingers in front of his face. "How would you like to be a test subject for a new virtual reality game?"

Charlie's eyes lit up. "Are you serious? That sounds amazing!"

Hollywood grinned. "I thought you'd like that. The company is called Neurotech, and they're looking for volunteers to try out their new VR system."

Charlie practically bounced in his seat with excitement. "When do I start?"

Hollywood chuckled. "Hold your horses, kid. You have to sign some waivers first. And there are some... risks involved."

Charlie's expression turned serious. "What kind of risks?"

Hollywood hesitated for a moment before answering. "There have been reports of people getting trapped in the simulation."

Charlie's enthusiasm waned slightly. "Like, they can't get out?"

Hollywood nodded gravely. "Yes. The technology is still experimental, and there are some kinks that need to be worked out."

Charlie chewed on his lip, thinking it over. Part of him was thrilled at the prospect of exploring a virtual world unlike anything he'd ever experienced before. But the thought of being stuck there indefinitely was terrifying.

"Can I think about it?" he asked finally.

"Of course," Hollywood said with a smile. "Take all the time you need. Just let me know what you decide."

Hollywood let out a deep sigh and leaned back in his chair, taking in the sight of his young protégé sitting across from him. Charlie was barely out of college, yet he had already made a name for himself with his sharp wit and quick thinking. Hollywood had taken notice of him early on and had decided to take him under his wing.

But now, as he looked at Charlie's crestfallen expression, Hollywood knew that he had to step up his game. He couldn't let this setback discourage the young man. "Listen, Charlie," he said, leaning forward. "I know it's tough, but you can't let this get you down."

Charlie looked up at him, his eyes filled with sadness. "But I thought I had it all figured out," he said. "I thought I was going to be a success."

Hollywood smiled gently. "You will be," he said. "You just need to keep moving forward."

Charlie nodded slowly, and Hollywood could see the determination returning to his eyes. "Okay," he said. "What's next?"

Hollywood grinned. "How about the world of fashion?" he suggested.

Charlie arched an eyebrow. "Fashion?" he repeated.

Hollywood nodded. "Yes, fashion," he said. "I know a guy who owns a clothing company and is looking for someone to help run it."

Charlie's face lit up with excitement. "That sounds amazing!" he exclaimed.

Hollywood chuckled. "I thought you'd like it," he said.

Your first house.

Hollywood & Charlie are in a trailer house.

Charlie: "Why are we in a trailer house?"

Hollywood: "You bought your first house it's too bad it'll roll down the hill every time the wind blows."

Chasity: "I wouldn't live here but then again I'm dead so if I could live again I would live anywhere."

Charlie: "Why did I buy a mobile home?"

Hollywood: "You're poor."

Charlie: "I'll have to change that."

Hollywood: "If you were related to your neighbors you could get a lot of pussy."

Chasity laughs and says "You have a sick mind."

Charlie rolls his eyes at Hollywood's comment and tries to change the subject. "So, what do you guys think of the town so far?" he asks.

Chasity shrugs. "It's a small town, not much to do."

Hollywood smirks. "Oh, I can think of a few things to do."

Chasity glares at him. "I swear you're disgusting."

Charlie clears his throat. "Let's just focus on fixing up this place, okay? It's not much, but it's ours."

Hollywood nods in agreement. "Yeah, we can make it work."

As the three of them get to work unpacking and organizing, Hollywood can't help but notice the way Chasity moves. She's graceful, beautiful even in her deathly state. He finds himself drawn to her.

Later that night, as Charlie heads to bed, Hollywood finds himself alone with Chasity.

"You know," he says slyly, "I may have a sick mind, but you intrigue me."

Chasity raises an eyebrow. "Is that so?"

Hollywood steps closer to her. "Yes. You're not like other girls I've met."

Chasity looks at him for a moment before leaning in and kissing him deeply. Hollywood is taken aback by her boldness, but he quickly responds to the kiss.

As they break apart for air, Hollywood can't help but feel drawn to her even more. He knows it's wrong on many levels – she's dead for one – but he can't resist her allure.

Charlie glared at Hollywood, his best friend who always seemed to have a crude remark ready at the tip of his tongue. He knew he couldn't let Hollywood's comment slide.

"That's not funny, man," Charlie said.

Hollywood shrugged. "I'm just stating the facts."

"You don't know anything about my neighbors," Charlie retorted.

"I bet they're all trailer park trash," Hollywood said with a smirk.

Chasity rolled her eyes. "Can we please stop talking about this? It's getting depressing."

Hollywood turned to her and grinned. "Well, if it makes you feel better, I happen to know a thing or two about making dead girls come alive."

Charlie could feel his cheeks flushing with anger. He stood up abruptly and pointed at the door. "Get out of my house, Hollywood. I don't want to hear another word from you."

Hollywood looked taken aback but then shrugged it off. "Suit yourself, man," he said as he sauntered out of the trailer.

Once he was gone, Charlie turned to Chasity. "I'm sorry you had to hear that."

"It's okay," she said with a sad smile. "I'm used to it by now."

Charlie chuckles and replies, "I think that's just Hollywood being Hollywood."

Hollywood winks at Charlie, "Hey, it's not my fault they're all hot and single."

Chasity interjects, "Well, I don't think you should be objectifying women like that. They are more than just objects for your pleasure."

Hollywood rolls his eyes, "Relax Chasity, it was just a joke. You know I respect women."

Charlie changes the subject, "So, what do you guys think about the new script I'm working on?"

Hollywood leans forward, intrigued. "Tell us more."

Charlie grins and begins explaining his latest project. As he speaks, his excitement grows and soon they are all fully invested in the story.

The hours pass by quickly as they discuss plot twists and character development. When they finally emerge from the trailer house, the sun is setting and they are all exhausted but exhilarated.

As they say their goodbyes for the night, Hollywood turns to Charlie with a smirk. "Hey man, maybe we can use that mobile home as a prop in the movie. It could add some authenticity to the low-budget vibe we're going for."

Charlie laughs, "You never know, Hollywood. Anything is possible in this crazy movie business."

Charlie raises his eyebrows and glances over at Hollywood, who just shrugs and grins. "What? It's true," he says.

Chasity rolls her eyes. "Boys will be boys," she mutters.

Charlie sighs and looks around the cramped trailer house. It's not exactly what he had dreamed of when he imagined owning his own home. But he's determined to make the best of it.

"I may be poor now, but I won't be forever," he says, more to himself than anyone else.

Hollywood nods. "That's the spirit. We'll brainstorm some ideas to get you rich."

Chasity smiles at Charlie. "I believe in you," she says.

Charlie feels a warmth spread through him at her words. He knows that Chasity is dead, but somehow it doesn't matter. In this moment, she feels more real than anyone else.

As they continue to chat and plan for the future, Charlie can't help but feel grateful for these two unlikely companions who have become his closest allies. And despite the less-than-ideal living situation, he knows that with their support, anything is possible.

Your first baby.

Hollywood & Charlie are in the hospital.

Charlie: "Why are we in the hospital?"

Hollywood: "You became a dad for the first time."

Chasity: "Oh how cute."

Charlie: "Which one is it?"

Hollywood: "The one on the end."

Chasity: "Damn Charlie made an ugly baby."

Hollywood: "That's an ugly little cum stain."

Charlie: "Hey watch it, that's my kid."

Hollywood: "It looks like it was born out of the wrong hole."

Charlie: "Is it a boy or a girl?"

Hollywood: "It looks like a hermaphrodite, hey it's the next Lady Gaga."

Charlie: "That's it, you like what you see."

Charlie: "You are a disgrace to the human family Hollywood, you ought to be put up for adoption."

Clarence and Jessica are in the gym on a weight machine.

Jessica: "Don't baby me like that again."

Clarence: "You are going to die on me if you don't start taking better care of yourself. I need you around here."

Jessica: "I have to admit it feels good knowing someone loves me enough to lose sleep over me."

Clarence: "Why do you think they call me Mr. Sensitive?"

Suddenly Jessica felt light headed and fell off the machine she was using.

Clarence caught her as she falls to the floor on top of him; Jessica turned white as sheet, she suddenly stopped breathing.

She had fainted from exhaustion combined with over training.

Clarence: "Damn girl, I told you take it easy with these machines; I look like a fool grabbing you falling all over me like this, we can get arrested for indecency for this shit talking about exercise at my age and your age isn't anything close to pretty. It's okay breath slow, deep breaths. Lord please let her live through this deadly humiliation we can't let anything happen to her she is our ticket to financial freedom. Daddy doesn't want no part of Obamacare's new health care plan just give us two more years and I'll be able to cover...

Chasity: "You did that on purpose?"

Charlie: "What?"

Hollywood: "Fucking that bitch fat head all the time."

Charlie: "Hey."

Hollywood: "She deliberately got knocked up so you could be stuck with her ugly ass kid the rest of your life."

Charlie: "Whoa, whoa, H-h-h-how would you know she did that, she didn't do that on purpose."

Hollywood: "Did you see what came out of her? You are going to be paying alimony and child support for the next twenty years and you are going to have nothing left, you fucking idiot. Your life is ruined after this shit. You better hope her mom paid for everything in cash because if not you are being robbed blind by her family."

Charlie: "You are just jealous because she likes me and not you. She is my baby mama now and I will see about a DNA test on that baby to prove it, son of a bitch."

Hollywood: "Get out of here then; I can't believe I was stupid enough to mentor your dumb ass this whole time, I should have just let you go to fucking jail like your best friend James. Whoa James, what's up? They let you out of jail early too, how's it feeling being a registered sex offender? Why don't you check every single one of us kids here for our registry information before we leave?

Charlie: "What's wrong with it?"

Hollywood: "The doctor says it's effeminate."

Charlie: "Well what did you expect, I grew up around a bunch of gay guys."

Hollywood: "This kid is gonna end up a mama's boy."

Charlie: "I blame my parents for this shit."

Hollywood: "You should go talk to your mom while she is still high and get a better dig on her."

Charlie: (to mom) "Why did you use to beat me?"

Mom: "What? what are you talking about? Hollywood beat you, he kicked you in the balls while I was fucking him for money. You were his punching bag slash sex toy when we were poor and hungry as hell." Hollywood: (to camera) "I forget that sometimes. If somebody mentioned it I wouldn't pay them any mind because it was so long ago and I was young and stupid sometimes, but I was like a fucking savage back then. Some people liked it, some hated it, but Charlie was there when I needed him and brought out the best in me more times than anybody else did and that's why I love him so much now cause I fucked him up so much as a child and he let me live with him now almost 30 years later. He was my only friend that totally understood everything about me in Hollywood in the early 80's and let me be who I am now.

Nurse: "Congratulations you are father."

Charlie: "Why is this thing breathing?"

Hollywood: "Just hold it and play with it. It will look less ugly in a few months anyway."

Charlie: "I guess so."

Hollywood: "It could be worse, partner. You could have been born with testicles in your mouth." "Like you, mother fucker?"

Charlie: "Yeah that is funny, but I am not holding it anymore. I can't wait to tell the gang at the bar about my kid... but first I have to change my clothes, so this baby shit doesn't stain my pants. Hollywood, take her/him/it to the nursery for me until I get ready to go home. Chasity (looking at baby): "So does this thing got a dick or vagina? Hollywood, do you know if its a dick or vagina? Because if it a dick then we can just call him Douglas.. and if its a vagina, then we will call it Dolores...Douglas or Dolores... yeah Dolores Douglas sounds good to me... so what do you think guys? We could make like a whole little nick name for it now - Dolorez Douglas. " Charlie comes out of the locker room in his street clothes before heading to the bar (he kicked everyone out of the room).

Charlie to nurse: "I am ready to go."

Nurse: "The father left with your baby already"

Your first wedding.

Hollywood & Charlie are watching Charlie's wedding.

Charlie: "Who is that I am marrying?"

Chasity: "It looks like an elephant in a wedding dress."

Hollywood: "That's Dan's sister."

Charlie: "Why the hell am I marrying her?"

Hollywood: "Maybe you like to 3 hole punch her or maybe you like how can lay on her stomach and pretend you're laying on a water bed."

Charlie: "Her pussy is like a cave."

Hollywood: "Yeah I know it's dark and scary when you walk around inside her but she's your wife now so man up."

Hollywood: "What about you Chasity you like sucking on Charlie's big black cock?"

Chasity: "I have one of my own."

Hollywood: "Wait I thought you were Dan's girlfriend."

Charlie: "You never have to do anything. Dan buys us clothes and pays for us to get our hair and nails done. He always takes care of us."

Hollywood: "I would never take care of you. You need to learn how to take care of yourself because what happens when Dan gets tired of your slutty ways, Then where will you be?"

Charlie: "We don't need boobs without nipples to take care of ourselves. It is amazing all the money we saved by not getting implants. We can spend it on a new set of tits if one of us loses a boob in a factory accident, like that would happened right Charlie? Or maybe he should marry a rich guy so we can have big fake tits, bus stop questions looks good for me."

Charlie: "The last time I was in jail I found someone girl who was sad because she lost one of her best friends and now I can only marry that girl even though she doesn't have two nuts but she still has a good lay. She's so good that I want her to marry my best friend who all he wants in life is to know if Charlie has twin girls or twin boys so at least he knew how many offspring that may sprout from him."

Charlie: "I can't even put it in this skinny bitch."

Hollywood: "Let me see that sex tape. Oh hell yeah! This is quality porn shit right here. Yea I would fuck her in the ass too!"

Then they both laughed and jerked off watching the scene where Dan is sliding his fat cock into Charlie's ass.

Peggy got off the phone and was mad. Peggy had called the wedding chapel to find out what room they were in and what flight number she was so pissed because she missed it. Peggy got a hotel room, changed clothes, and used her old key to open Charlie's door. Peggy thought when she heard him moaning and saw them fucking on the bed that they could have just invited her.

Chasity: "You would know because you like to walk around her like you're a caveman."

Hollywood: "Charlie, you need to work on your whole package."

Charlie: "But why would any man want you? You're just a housewife. The only thing men want from you is sex and someone to wipe their ass."

Hollywood: "I look for my marriage partner in the same place I found my husband, prison."

Charlie: " That doesn't make sad at all! So they're equal in your eyes? So if I go there I might find someone just as good as that big ass Marilyn-looking bitch in the wedding dress who just happens to look like 50 shades of Gray. Chasity (voice over): They were two assholes talking shit about me while I was making eggplant Parmesan and massaging his feet because his back is hurting from the strain between my thighs and his man made me give him a full body massage every day but it was all on the down-low because we have unwritten rules on this shit.

Hollywood: "Hey, did you and Marilyn make a baby yet?"

Hollyweird kissing Charlie's foot thinking he doesn't want to pay child support.

Charlie: "Idk, maybe, maybe not. I never have a condom on me when she tries to get pregnant. I don't make that much money so the thought of paying for a kid scares me.

Your first honeymoon.

Hollywood & Charlie are in the hotel room on Charlie's honeymoon while Charlie & Fat Girl have over the top sex.

Charlie: "Holy hell she's crushing me."

Chasity: "That's a sight I didn't want to see."

Hollywood: "Her pussy is hungry and it's gonna eat you."

Charlie: "Someone call the zoo and get that horny hippo off me."

Hollywood: "At least she was born a woman and even though she's fat and ugly, she still probably has better pussy than Tara Reid."

Charlie: "How does that help me?"

Hollywood: "Just picture Megan Fox when you're fucking her."

Charlie: "I'd rather not picturing anyone because it really never lives up to what I imagine."

Hollywood: "Would you rather be in a room watching it with me? I mean, in all fairness I could have at least rubbed one out first but I didn't think about it until it was too late."

Charlie: "Well, if that hippo had any rhythm she could probably use it as a sexual weapon."

Hollywood: "If we get our ass kicked I'm blaming you." Charlie: "What for? I came to a whore hotel for fucking, that's what we got."

Hollywood: "But they said they were going to kill us."

Charlie: "Well along time ago people said prostitutes were going to kill off porno. Well that didn't happen and neither will this. Plus, if you die you get to fuck Genevieve Bosse in the next life so don't worry about it, just over think it. Besides, how are they gonna find us, everybody has sex here pretty much all the time. It stinks like bacon and pussy. You can smell the room a mile away from the front door and they STILL call this asshole an "Adults Only" hotel."

Hollywood: "Okay, but if anything happens beneath this sheet I'm blaming you again. Plus my nuts are wising up to these heels.

Charlie: "I already fucked her."

Later, Charlie has a chance encounter with a bus full of showgirls.

One of the showgirls is Pamela Anderson wearing a bra and panties (thanks to Tara Reid) and she asks Charlie if he wants to play some games.

Hollywood, struggling to find a bathroom for himself: Why does every guy's fantasy have to include Showgirls?

Charlie: "Because that scene was the most awesome thing I've ever seen on film before I fucked Roxanne . . . wait the hell up, don't flush it! I've got to pee!"

Lost Lake, Las Vegas, NV:

At a pool party at this casino/hotel Tara Reid begins her journey to find love with Grinder boy-toy. She does not remember his name, but she will make sure everyone else knows it with Grinder tattoos. Neck, waist, ass and arm on command just because he loves her so much . . . anything for you baby. She then asks for the return of her heart shaped glasses from Mike Tyson – who was out of them for over 10 days. Problem ?! No matter their sorry situation comedians are making jokes about it as they walk past.

Doreen: "You don't just lose somebody's heart glasses, especially when they are Converse Chuck Taylors!"

Charlie: "She has both of us in and it's so tight I'm afraid."

Hollywood: "Don't mind her, she's just practicing for Black Monday."

Charlie: "We have to get out of here, we shouldn't see this. I was born into this but you won the ticket off a waiver wire!"

Hollywood: "I know she isn't the smallest when she's dry but, my god, that looks like some young Russian man down there. She could give Vlady Pushka a run for his money. She is bottomless! And what the hell is up with all of that hair? I have never seen a lava lamp like that in my life!"

Charlie: "Let me see yours (points to Hollywood)

Hollywood: "No way dude, you are fucking her right now remember?"

Charlie: "Come on, let me see your wiener! Ease my mind a bit here! Just look at hers and then you will know yours isn't so bad."

Hollywood: "No way dude, you are her first husband so it wouldn't be right! Besides, I'm afraid it might break off from all of its fat. It's probably used to being inside fat girls so little Charlie here maybe a bit too tight of a fit. Looks like she would be good at muff diving though.

Charlie: "It's not that easy."

Hollywood: "Picture Megan Fox naked."

Charlie: "I don't need to picture Megan Fox naked. I know she looks like a mud flap."

Hollywood: "Look, she just offered me her right ass cheek so get off the couch and mount that zebra."

Charlie: "I don't need to watch this and I can't believe you want me to watch this. This is disgusting. I can smell her from here. A fucking hippo will go extinct before Fat Girl gets back into her wedding dress. We gotta start making our move tonight or it's over. We gotta get the band back together and start hunting Bigfoot and stuff so what do you say, boss? You in? Let's go kill some Bigfoot? I wouldn't even blame you if you bailed after seeing what happened in there tonight. Fuck, I was tempted to bail myself. Damnit, Hollywood...Brasil...where are you? Now that we got the money, it's time for Charlie MacKenzie to retire and work on opening Phoenix House rehab center for freaks like us! Cops don't have to worry if their kids go out with freaks if they got a house for them to live in, right? And then while those freaks are staying with us at Phoenix House rehab center for freaks, we screw all of them! Peace out amigos!

Your first holiday at the in laws.

Charlie is sitting at the table with Fat Girl & Dan on thanksgiving.

Dan: "Guess what I did last night?"

Hollywood: "Got ass fucked by a donkey."

Chasity: "Oh gross." Laughs.

Charlie: "Tested positive for stupid."

Dan: "No, I had a 3some with Amanda Bynes and Rihanna."

Hollywood: "I would fuck both of these girls but I think he somehow got them confused with his left and right hands."

Chasity: "He has a fun imagination."

Charlie: "Sure you did and last week I won the lottery in 5 states while fucking Angelina Jolie , Jessica Alba and Halle Berry."

Dan: "Okay, okay, don't rub it in."

Hollywood: "You need to go to France... so that your dick could actually fuck a Frenchie."

Chasity: "Shh! Stop talking like that. Women are in the house. Can you imagine if there were guys here?"

Fat Girl: "It doesn't bother me. I had my first when I was fifteen. It was pretty embarrassing with my dad sitting beside me and everything but I did manage to get an A on my health class essay about sexually transmitted diseases. Then again, the only partner I had was Justin Beiber . The depression made it hard for him to perform well in bed, he kinda just laid there and sobbed most of the time leaving me unfulfilled and unsatisfied."

Everybody Laughs except Dan because he quickly figures out how stupid that little story was.

Dan: "So, Charlie, you like Thanksgiving right?"

Charlie: "I guess, thanksgiving is cool... I love pumpkin pie."

Everybody Laughs except for Charlie... he is just confused and shocked by this asshole named Dan making fun of him.

Fat Girl: "So do you have any plans? Your mom doesn't have anything planned for us right? She doesn't make you do anything crazy before she gets home from work or anything?" Charlie feigns horror as this question is asked and why does this girl who used to sit next door to us in health class always make such ....

Dan: "I swear it happened."

Hollywood: "Really...you're laying in the afterglow of your second threesome and all you can think about is telling everyone about it when a glass of water is literally what you need."

Dan: "You should fuck both of them, man."

Hollywood: "I'd rather lick the sweat off my asshole than have sex with either one of them."

Look at Charlie's face, then look back 10 seconds and he's finally laughing. He has to see Dan is out of fucking gas to even make fun of his absurd statement. The only thing I want to know is how they'd get that marquee before those windows go black with a projection made from Dan's mind calling out his pitchman lines and asking if anyone wants to guess what my sandwich is?

Dan: "Really, is that what you go to school for."

Charlie: "No actually collection agencies."

Dan: "Wish I had gone to school for that."

Hollywood: "Haha haha what a jackass. By the way Halley is coming over later, you can watch her burn shit down while we play with smores. All this talk about fucking girls made me hungry. Do you know where the Brownies are?"

Charlie: "I'll check the back of the Fat Girls ass."

Fat Girl: "Fuck you Charlie!"

Charlie: "Fuck you too Amanda Bynes."

Everyone ran there separate ways as Dan began yelling at Chasity in his basement again about finger cots and spoons but that is neither here or there *see what I did there*. When Hollywood & Charlie got to his house, he had one of those big metal trashcans fire on the porch full of wet leaves, empty cans that had held beer and a few boxes that read things like "Do Not Throw Out" , "Keep This For Future Use", "Nevermind". Charlie helped Galaxy put it all on a cardboard box and set it on fire with some lighter fluid they found next to the cans. As they stood watching the fire, Hollywood said/said loudly "It could be hours before those brownies burn."

Charlie: "Hey lay off it would be hours before she spread more blankets on your bed in a star-fishing position wearing nothing but boots.

Your first divorce.

Hollywood & Charlie watch as Charlie gets a divorce.

Dan: "Hey Charlie, guess what I did last night?"

Hollywood: "Gave Darren a reach around."

Chasity laughs.

Charlie: "I'm guessing you didn't win an IQ contest."

Dan: "No, I went to the playboy mansion and had sex with every woman there."

Chasity: "What dream world does he live in?"

Hollywood: "I think he meant to say is he went to the trailer park and had sex with his relatives."

Charlie: "Dan, you are the biggest liar I've ever met, you probably dildoed your mangina last night."

Dan then chases Charlie around the kitchen, Returns to normal. Hollywood and Chasity watch as Dan continues to act like a murder suspect who acted normally when found guilty...

Hollywood: "Charlie stop moving you're making Dan need to murder someone and he dildoed his mangina really hard."

Charlie runs around the counter top into the freezer. The cops walk in at that moment because somebody just called 911 from the house and Hunk Warrior and Charlisa are sitting at the table eating a ham sandwich watching as the cops cuff Charlie and take him away.

Hollywood & Chasity: "What happened?"

Officers: "Your friend is being arrested for murdering one of our detectives and stuffing him in an ice box."

Chasity: "Oh...well I'm sure if we put an Alibi video on Youtube he'll be out in no time."

Later that day...

Hollywood: "Congratulations Charlisa your uncle Charlie will be out of jail in only 15 minutes which means Charlisa has 2-3 days away from you, how exciting."

Charlisa: "I don't know why but I feel like something really bad is going to happen tonight so you three better not be here when it does."

Everybody grins while staring at her. She stares right back at them in fear as they begin showing off their 55 inch flat screen TV's and surround sound speakers for their own home entertainment systems...

Dan: "No, I have a girlfriend right now, and we just had sex then I went right into the studio to record."

Charlie: "So you sent her to the studio. Was your hand broken or what? What is wrong with you? Who sends their girlfriend to the studio?"

Hollywood shakes his head and looks at the camera guy.

Chasity is laughing hysterically.

Charlie: "I did that once, where is my trophy. You want a trophy Dan? I would name it but you would never remember it."

The front door of the office opens, then closes loudly. I tune out of the conversation when I see it's Lou coming in frowning at everyone and heading behind the bar. When he's finished stacking glasses he goes over to Kari leaning against the bar and wraps his arms around her waist holding her tight against him drumming his fingers up and down her hips. Lou meets my gaze briefly before returning to his conversation with Kari.

Chasity: "What's going on with Lou lately, he seems pissed off more than usual?"

Hollywood: "Yeah, I think he has a bone to pick with someone."

Charlie: "He has always been a grumpy old man, upsets me when he wants to kiss me yet still tries to bite me off."

I grin at Charlie winking at him and start pulling a clean glass down from the shelf by our heads that only restaurant workers can reach without scaffolding holding them up for..

Charlie looks at Hollywood.

Hollywood: "I live vicariously through that guy, I have yet to grow a set to try and kill someone and want you to know that my friend is nothing but a fat heartless bastard who couldn't load up a cart with enough food to fill an ant farm."

Dan grabs his chest.

Dan: "Oh my heart hurts!"

Charlie kicks the chair out from under Dan.

Charlie: "Okay, time for your pills!"

Teacher: "Attention class, I know it isn't Friday."

Waking up.

Charlie wakes up in his bed.

Charlie groans and opens his eyes. He's in his own bed, in his bedroom. It's a sunny Saturday morning. He's not sure what day it is, but he knows he has some chores to do before turning on his game console.

Charlie can see the window, the light from outside illuminating the particles floating in the air, his desk, his computer screen and the keyboard.

The room is the same as it's always been. Same sheets, same furniture, same outlets, same posters dot the walls in a staggered pattern. Same tangles of wires in the floor, same dust in the air. Same streetlamp through the window, same street below.

Charlie smells a hint of cinnamon and the must or dust. He doesn't like to clean his room, he'll probably have to vacuum it later.

The room smells of dank cotton sheets, fresh laundry, and Charlie's aftershave.

The room smells like his mother's cooking from the day before.

Charlie's tongue feels the toothpaste, like toothpaste, and nothing else.

His taste buds wake up to the feel of a cottony pillow and silky sheets.

Charlie hears his mother downstairs, he knows she's still asleep. He doesn't want to wake her because she'll start her day. Later he'll sneak downstairs and make her a cup of coffee.

Charlie hears the birds outside, the hum of his computer fan, and the soft patter of rain from the weather outside.

Charlie hears his mother's footsteps on the floor above, along with the shifting of furniture and the loud thump of his brother's door closing.

Charlie feels the softness of his white sheets and the coolness of the breeze coming in from the window. He'll open the window and let in the fresh air.

Charlie feels his bed's silky sheets, the soft pillow, the cold metal of his alarm clock.

The bed is soft like he'd come to expect, the covers are comfortable and welcomed.

Charlie awakens tired, confused, and still a little drunk, unsure where he is or how he got here. On the bedside table is a half-empty bottle of Zubrowka, a tiny crystal statue of a knight, a brass model of a horse and rider. The walls are a stark white, beneath stark white trim. He is in a strange room, one he cannot place. After a couple of minutes, he remembers his name and stretches, a deep yawn, a contraction of old tendons in his back and neck.

New understanding.

Charlie comes to a new understanding about his life.

Charlie is sitting in a chair facing the window.

Charlie looks in the mirror. Hello. His reflection stares back at him. Fear washes over him. He flees his reflection. He closes his eyes. Charlie opens his eyes. And stares back at himself.

Charlie walked through the house, every inch of it familiar to him like his own face. He could identify different rooms and furnishings with ease. He knew every crevice in the walls, every stain on the ceiling, every blemish on the wooden floors. He could trace the clean lines of the walls and still know when they were repainted, when the house was remodeled. And yet, everything looked different.

The aroma of fresh-cut flowers nips at Charlie's nose. He is in Lilac Park. He looks around. He sees lilac bushes. He turns his head. And sees a garden of beautiful flowers, like roses.

The smell of sawdust and old wood stung his nostrils. Even if he hadn't felt the sawdust under his nails he knew he'd done some carpentry in his day. The smell was there.

Charlie can hear the insects chirping. And the trees swaying in the breeze.

The chair is made of wood and is very uncomfortable for Charlie.

Charlie feels the lilac's texture. They feel like warm fuzzy blankets. He feels the soft grass crunching beneath his feet. And the air is just as soft.

Charlie ran his hands along the grooves in the wood of the bookshelves carved by hand. He glanced at the photos on the walls – some hanging crooked, some with the corners curling off – and traced fingers along the frames.

New job.

Charlie gets a new job at a large company.

The sign on the front of the building is 32 feet long, the words in ornate script and the logo in a woodcut style. The building is brick, built in the late 1920's. It has two stories, with the upper story glassed in. The windows are large.

Charlie is old and gray, but he drives the elevator like there's no tomorrow. He's in charge of the whole building now, he is the man.

Charlie's new company, SolidFrog, is located in a large skyscraper. It takes him almost an hour to get to work in the morning, driving with the other employees, at least 40 of them.

The air in the room is stale and musty, like too many people in a closed room for too long.

Charlie's breath is like a Christmas tree: sharp, tangy, a hint of pine.

The air above the city smells like skunk; the odor from the subway below.

There is a click of the door, a rustle of clothes and a scuff of shoes on the marble floors. There is a low rumble of voices from the hall as the other office workers talk, the walls muffling the sound into a low droning.

Charlie's voice is the sound of a metronome, a clock, hisses and ticks and clicks and clacks.

When Charlie arrives at work, he decides to park in the back of the lot instead of the front, like he used to.

Charlie's voice is a buttery deep, like a buttered and toasted slice of toast.

The chair is leather, the desk is smooth, the watch on your wrist is chrome and your shoes are polished and shined.

Charlie has calloused hands and an iron grip from years of working on cars as a mechanic. He's not afraid to get dirty.

Charlie is contacted by a recruiter through email. He eventually accepts a position as a programmer, after a few weeks of negotiations and some informal interviews. The email is form letter, but Charlie likes the idea of working in a large company like SolidFrog. A sense of accomplishment floods him.

New house.

Charlie moves out of the apartment into his new house.

Charlie stood at the threshold of his new house, taking in a deep breath. He had been saving for this moment for months, and the reality of it had not yet quite sunk in. He imagined the future he would have here: the late-night talks he would have with friends on the porch, the laughter echoing through the halls of the house, the sweet smell of freshly-baked cookies emanating from the kitchen.

He looked back at his old apartment building one last time. After months of scraping together enough money to make the down payment, he had a place of his own at last. He felt a pang of sadness at leaving his old life behind, but he knew that he was ready to start anew.

He lifted his bags, stepped through the doorway, and closed the door behind him. He was home.

New girl.

Fade out with Charlie meeting a new girl.

Hollywood & Chasity stand in the background smiling and disappear.

As the sun set over the city, Charlie walked slowly along the bustling sidewalks, taking in the sights and sounds of the gathering night. He was on his way to a school dance, the first one he had been to in months. His mind whirred with the possibilities, and he felt an unmistakeable thrill of anticipation at the thought of all the new connections he was about to make.

Along the way, his eyes fell on a group of people standing off to the side of the street. He slowed his pace, drawn in by the sight of them, and he noticed with a start that among them was a young woman who was strikingly beautiful. She had glossy dark hair that framed her face and a warm, inviting smile. Charlie felt his heart beating faster as their eyes met, and he knew without a doubt that this was someone he wanted to get to know better.

He took a few steps closer to the group and saw that the young woman was surrounded by two other people, both of whom Charlie recognized from his school. One of them, Hollywood, gave Charlie a friendly wave and the other, Chasity, smiled broadly at him.

"Hey there," Charlie said as he approached, his voice strangely quiet. "The dance is starting soon. Do you want to go together?"

The young woman's smile widened, and she nodded her head in agreement.

"Yes," she said. "That would be great."

Charlie felt a wave of relief wash over him, and he smiled back at her. Hollywood and Chasity stepped back and away from the pair, disappearing into the crowd. Together, Charlie and the young woman began the journey to the dance, neither of them aware of what the night ahead would bring.

The End.

Don't miss out!

Visit the website below and you can sign up to receive emails whenever Aaron Abilene publishes a new book. There's no charge and no obligation.

https://books2read.com/r/B-A-YOIP-OSLNC

BOOKS 2 READ

Connecting independent readers to independent writers.

Also by Aaron Abilene

505
505: Resurrection

Balls
Dead Awake

Carnival Game
Full Moon Howl
Donovan
Shades of Z

Deadeye
Deadeye & Friends
Cowboys Vs Aliens

Ferris
Life in Prescott

Afterlife in Love

Island
Paradise Island
The Lost Island
The Lost Island 2
The Island 2

Pandemic
Pandemic

Prototype
The Compound

Slacker
Slacker 2
Slacker: Dead Man Walkin'

Texas
A Vampire in Texas

Thomas
Quarantine

Contagion
Eradication
Isolation

Zombie Bride
Zombie Bride
Zombie Bride 2
Zombie Bride 3

Standalone
The Victims of Pinocchio
A Christmas Nightmare
Pain
Fat Jesus
A Zombie's Revenge
505
The Headhunter
Crash
Tranq
The Island
Dog
The Quiet Man
Joe Superhero
Feral
Good Guys
Devil Child of Texas
Romeo and Juliet and Zombies
The Gamer
Becoming Alpha
Dead West

Small Town Blues

The Gift of Death

Killer Claus

Home Sweet Home

Alligator Allan

10 Days

Army of The Dumbest Dead

Kid

The Cult of Stupid

9 Time Felon

Slater

Me Again

Maurice and Me

Sparkles The Vampire Clown

She's Psycho

Vicious Cycle

Romeo and Juliet: True Love Conquers All

Random Acts of Stupidity

The Abducted

Graham Hiney

The Firsts in Life